greasewood creek

a novel

greasewood creek

PAMELA STEELE

COUNTERPOINT
BERKELEY

Library of Congress Cataloging-in-Publication data is available.

ISBN 978-1-58243-770-5

Cover design by Natalya Balanova
Interior design by www.meganjonesdesign.com
Printed in the United States of America

COUNTERPOINT
1919 Fifth Street
Berkeley, Ca 94710

www.counterpointpress.com

Distributed by Publishers Group West

10 9 8 7 6 5 4 3 2 1

greasewood creek

greasewood creek

THE AIR STILL holds the shape of the house. August light pushes through cottonwood limbs—no more than air themselves—shimmers off ghost windows. Weed-shot grass seeps from the empty pasture, scabs over the ground where the house once sat, surrounds a shard of foundation. Beneath this scab, a wound of rust and ash—years of dirt sifted through porch boards, glass, the crumbling razor blades Frank dropped through cracks in the bathroom floor.

A south wind sizzles through the dry grass, brushes Avery's bare legs, rises into the limbs of the cottonwoods. It surges through a swath of apple trees to the east, whispers the names of her sister, grandmother, father before it rushes north across the pasture toward the only other house she's lived in—the place Paul and Mary left to Davis, their only grandchild.

Across the distance, she makes out the shape of the house, the wind-battered sheds and barn, the blue blur of Davis's F-150 parked in the yard, and next to it, Lovell's red International. She guesses the fencing is done—that Lovell has stayed to talk—pictures them sitting on the back porch drinking the last of this morning's coffee or maybe whiskey from the bottle Lovell keeps behind his truck seat.

In the orchard, threads of light fall between leaves of sixty-year-old trees, catch on dusty apple skin. Avery reaches into lower limbs, twists glowing planets out of their orbits, drops them into a pillowcase, each apple a reminder of Grandma and Grandpa Coleman, of seedlings carried on Grandma's lap as they rode the train to Eastern Oregon from West Virginia.

As Avery raises her arms, muscle memory sparks—makes her a child again—then it is her father Frank who lifts her into the loose nets of spiderwebs and drifting motes, lifts her toward the apples, calls their names: Wolf River, Guinea, Red June.

When the pillowcase is half full, Avery starts back to the Jeep, steps into horizontal light at the edge of the orchard. Wind stirs rye grass anchored in the far slope of the dry irrigation ditch. The low light shifts, bends itself into water that fills the ditch again, catches on dry stems, makes them her sister's pale hair floating on the current. Time pulls Avery back across the years to a June day, to the hum of her mother's washing machine on the porch. She hears the sound of Madeline's voice across the yard. Words surface from memory. She hears her say, Avery, keep an eye on your sister!

june 1970

THE DAY, A blade of yellow light spreading through the wheatfield, carving the edges of Table Rock clean from the sky. The backyard is muddy and lush, the vein of the irrigation ditch dark with rain and snowmelt.

Avery and Jean Ann on the backporch, playing house. Madeline, just inside the door, slamming the washing machine lid, saying through the screen, Avery, keep Jean Ann on that porch!

Jean Ann lies on the porch swing, pretends to take a nap. We're having spinach for dinner, Avery says. Jean Ann cracks open an eye, scrunches her face, sticks out her tongue. Avery tiptoes down the porch steps, stuffs a fistful of grass into a canning jar, dips the jar into a puddle. As she does, she hears the screendoor squeak, hears her mother say, Get out of that mud and get up on this porch. If I catch you down there again, I'm going to wear you out!

Now, Madeline in the yard, jerking the jar from Avery's hands, dumping the grass and muddy water, squeezing Avery's arm. Hard. Stay away from that water, she says.

On the porch, Avery moves near Jean Ann's face, counts to five. Jean does not move. Avery walks to the edge of the porch, listens, waits for Jean Ann to stop pretending, to call her back, but there is only the sound of the washer.

At the clothesline, she waits again, this time to hear her mother's voice, to feel the sting of a palm on her bare leg, but there is nothing. She looks back at the house once, pushes past a damp bedsheet, lets it fall, lets it muffle the sound of the ditch. Lets it make her invisible.

In the garden, she pulls yellow leaves off peavines, flicks ants off a peony bud, pries open its knot of pink-white petals. She drops them, watches them float to the ground. Now her fingers smell like her mother's face cream.

THEN, MADELINE'S VOICE—a shout. Avery freezes, watches a black ant zigzag across her knuckles. Her mother's voice again. Avery turns toward the clothesline, stretches her arms, pushes through. The thin, blue sheet brushes her head and neck, makes a little breeze down the backs of her legs, as if someone is standing behind her.

Across the yard, Madeline, like she has dropped a pile of wet clothes on the ditch bank, like she is trying to gather them up into her arms again.

Now, Avery can see—sees her mother pulling her sister into her lap. A net of hair, gone dark from muddy water, yellow T-shirt, red shorts. Jean Ann's bare feet, legs the color of ashes. Avery stops walking, she cannot breathe. The air becomes thick, a cushion of heat around her.

Avery watches her mother's face, pale, mouth stretched wide like she might scream again, but there is no sound—only the water slipping through the ditch. Madeline rocks on her heels, tears the hair away from Jean Ann's face, then stops, lays her on the ground. She crouches over Jean Ann, lays the side of her face against the T-shirt, listens, her eyes squeezed shut, then she sits up, puts her fingers against Jean Ann's neck, rolls her onto her side, slaps her back with the flat of her hand, making a sound like pounding dough on the bread-board. A small ribbon of dark water slips out of Jean Ann's mouth.

Madeline stands, her knees grass-stained and muddy, her own feet bare. She picks up Jean Ann again, holds her against her own body, lurches toward the house. Passes Avery, does not look at her. At the porch steps, she stumbles, lurches, stumbles again. She opens the screendoor with her foot and they are gone.

At the top of the steps, dark outlines of water drops spread into the porch boards. Avery follows them, stands at the screendoor, the slamming sound still in her head, the smell of metal and fly spray strong in her nose. Avery watches through the mesh. Her mother lays Jean Ann on the couch, then pulls an afghan over her, kneels on the floor near Jean Ann's head. She fusses with the wet hair.

Avery wants her father. She turns to see if he might be coming home. She looks out over the yard, finds it changed. The light bouncing off the sheets on the clothes-line hurts her eyes. The trees have moved closer, the sky farther away. Grandma Coleman's voice, from a day not long before, comes into her head, You got to help your mama out, Avery. Look after your sister.

Avery scans the road, the field for her father. She stands on the porch, staring down into the cup of one purple iris, levitating among the green spears by the cement foundation. When the sound from her mother comes like steam rushing out of a teakettle, she wobbles back down the stairs, crawls under the porch, stunned, ashamed.

She has let her sister drown.

telling

LAST NIGHT, A storm. This morning, the barn hunkered in the pasture—flayed animal—rain-soaked, side door flapped open on loose hinges. Before daylight, the clouds moved away, a third-quarter moon sprayed light onto strips of tin hanging from its roof, onto the hood of Davis's pickup as he drove off to Obsidian Springs to shoe horses.

All morning, Avery hauled shattered limbs in the wheelbarrow, dumped them on the burn pile. Now, she peels corral poles Davis and Lovell brought down from the hills yesterday.

The lodgepole is dry this time of year, hard to peel. Over and over, she pulls the drawknife toward her with both hands, works down the length of wood, turns it to expose unpeeled bark, starts again.

She thinks of Lovell, wonders if there was not thirty-two years' difference in their ages, whether she might have loved him. She does love him, but it might have been in a different way. She thinks of the first time she met him, just after her mother had given her over to Mary, just after her father vanished into the air of the wheatfield.

THE MORNING SHE first sees Lovell, he sits on a kitchen chair close to the edge of Paul and Mary's porch, head down, turning a piece of wood in his hands. The way the denim goes lighter at the knees of his jeans startles her, makes her think of her father, whom she hasn't seen in weeks. The man sits much higher in the chair than Frank did. She looks at the top of his head, white threads of hair. Not her father.

She steps on the bottom step and the man looks up. His eyes are blue, near to the color of the bachelor buttons that poke up between the broken trucks in the back pasture. He smiles. The lines rippling out from the sides of his mouth make Avery think of water after a stone has dropped into it.

Hello, there, he says, not loud, not soft, but the way she heard her father talk to the lady who works in the bank.

She walks to the top of the steps, stands in front of him, says nothing. He is still looking at her.

Not much of a talker, are you?

Avery knows this is not a question, but the way his words come out do not sound mean.

I'm Lovell. I help Paul out sometimes. I got a little girl about your age. Six, are you?

This time, it *is* a question. Rude not to answer, but all she can manage is a nod.

Thought so.

He hands her the piece of wood then pulls a small knife out of his shirt pocket. She studies the wood, runs her fingers over it, feels the weight of it like a living thing in her hand.

I come from West Virginia, same as your folks. Mary, too. You and I aren't kin, I don't think.

Lovell opens the knife, wipes both sides of the blade on the leg of his jeans. He holds his hand out toward her.

OK, I'll take that back now.

His hand is scratched up, missing the tip of the index finger. The rest of the fingers are flat on the ends, look like they have been smashed and never gone back to their right shapes. She gives him the piece of wood, lifts her hand to her nose, recognizes the smell of the trees down by the river.

Cottonwood, he says. He lays the knife handle across his palm, starts scratching at the wood with it.

This here is the head, he says, nodding at one end of the chunk of wood. The best end of a horse.

She can hear the smile in his voice.

Curls of wood drift onto the floorboards, the rough toes of his boots. You gonna tell me your name?

Avery, she says.

Avery, he repeats. My girl is Lennie. She lives with me most of the time, but right now, she's staying over on the Indian reservation with her mother. Be home before school starts. You start school this year, too?

Now, the curls of wood are finer, and because of the breeze, they drift off the porch, into the flower bed, lie on the petals like yellow worms.

How do you make that? Avery asks, pointing at his work.

Pretty simple, he says. You just take away everything that ain't the horse. He grins. Bachelor buttons, stone in water.

Avery's jacket is pitch-splattered, her arms sore by the time she hears Davis's pickup in the driveway. He comes around the shed, grins when he sees the peeled posts.

You smell like Christmas, he tells her.

After supper, they stand on the back porch, watch a line of blackbirds lift from a telephone wire over the road. Dark shapes scatter like buckshot over the pasture, regroup, settle in the dry stubble of the wheatfield. Birds are gathering up, Davis says, Sign of cold weather.

In thin afternoon light, Avery holds a ladder while Davis nails the loose tin back onto the barn. I want to say something to you when you get down, she says.

She waits at the bottom of the ladder, her back to the wind that picks up again. When Davis comes down, she steps away from him, faces him. The cold air has brought up the color in his pale skin. She reaches into his jacket pocket, takes out the elkskin glove he's stuck in there. She pulls it back onto his right hand, says, I guess you know I'm pregnant.

Then, a moment of waiting. The wind tears at her scarf, pushes against the back of her jacket. She registers the ache in her own hands from gripping the ladder frame while Davis stood on it.

She watches his eyebrows rise. He grins. He folds her into him, against his warmth, his breath in her ear. She hears—feels—him inhale, smelling her hair, her neck, like he always does when he holds her like this.

You sure? he asks. When?

Yep. The last week of May, probably. Thereabouts.

Hmmm, he says into her shoulder. He pushes her away, then opens his coat, pulls her inside it. We have, what, eight months or so?

Yep, a little more, she says. Lennie says I—everything—looks fine.

His mouth is at her ear again, his breath moist in the wool of her hat. I suppose you'll want Lennie to see you through this—want her to deliver you at home, he says.

Over Davis's shoulder, the sky is nearly dark, but she can see the storm-stripped line of cottonwoods by the irrigation ditch. She remembers what Davis once told her about the trees on the Plateau, pointing out something she should have noticed, but hadn't. Here, in fall, he'd said, the trees always shed their leaves in this order: locust, cottonwood, then oak. One of the dependable things in this world.

I don't want to find out whether it's a boy or girl until it gets here, she says.

Good, he says. Me, neither.

Inside the house, they take off their boots, lay scarves and gloves on the kitchen table, go into the darkened living room to lie down on the couch together.

Davis pulls his hand through Avery's hair. She smells the Lava soap on his skin and the scent of her own hair on the couch pillow, left there after this morning's nap.

Somewhere above them, attic windows shudder. She feels the roughness of Davis's wool sock against her ankle, is aware of the exact shape of the place on her back where her shirt has ridden up, where cold air brushes her skin. *All of this, all of this*, she thinks, because there is someone else in the room with them, and just now, between them.

june 1973

THE TOP SHEET is light, cool on Avery's skin. It gathers heat from her shoulders and arms, gathers the smell of shaving cream—Mary's sunburn cure.

Today, she helped Mary pick bugs off tomatoes, pull weeds from rows of onions and cabbage, asked about the plastic owl hanging in the tree at the edge of the garden.

Paul ordered that thing from the Fingerhut catalog, Mary said. Supposed to scare away birds—keep them from eating the seeds. I guess it works, she laughed.

Cool air sifts through the window screen. With it, the sound of engines out on the main road, disappearing into long twilight. Avery listens for her mother's muffler—knows she won't hear it. Madeline stopped coming to get her after sundown a while ago—has almost stopped coming for her at all.

From the front room, muffled sounds: the tv, clock chime, Paul hacking up hay dust. From the kitchen, the oven door, opening then closing, water running in the sink. Mary's puttering, getting ready. Tomorrow, her daughter Caroline will drive in from Idaho, leaving her boy Davis to stay through haying season.

WHAT GRADE YOU in? he asks. He tips his glass, drinks the last of the Kool-Aid.

Going to fourth, she says. What grade are you in?

Sixth, he says.

Above them, locust leaves twist in the hot breeze. Avery picks hay stems out of her shoelaces, still feels the throb of the tractor in her calves and feet.

You stay here all the time? he asks.

A red crescent of Kool-Aid above his top lip. Flecks of dried blood and hay in the fine blond hair on his arms.

Most of the time, she says. My mom stays gone a lot.

He picks at a scab on his arm. I heard about your sister, he says.

Needles of sweat in the hay scratches on her own arms. She says, Where's your dad?

Army, he says. Vietnam.

Oh, she says, thinks about the news on Paul's tv, the black-and-white picture propped on the front room shelf, the smiling, beautiful Caroline, a man in uniform beside her, the blond, toothless boy anchored to his knee. She asks him, When's he coming home?

He shrugs, says, Where's your grandma and grandpa?

Dead, she says. My Grandma Coleman just died this winter. My dad's mom and dad are dead, too. Before I was born.

willow

O N THE RIVERBANK, red twigs, pieces of blue baling twine—blood vessels against a thin skin of snow. Lennie hands Avery the knife, says, Hold this a minute. Watch out, it's pretty sharp. She wiggles her index finger inside the glove, says, It's how Dad cut the tip of his finger off, cutting willow for Mom.

Just teach me how to make the cradle, Avery says. I'll try not to cut my finger off.

Yeah, Lennie says, points to Avery's belly. If you get hurt, Davis will have my hide. He's pretty protective of both of you now that you're pregnant.

I know, Avery says. He watches me like he thinks I'm going to disappear. She doesn't say that sometimes, while she waits for Davis to come home in the evenings, she sits in the kitchen and imagines the child rolling and shifting inside her. She senses the quickness of the baby's heartbeats filling the spaces between her own, the sound called up from the memory of Lennie holding the feto-scope to her ear.

She doesn't say that when the house is quiet and weak light washes through the window, fear comes over her—a fear she cannot name. She knows she should be happy—is happy—but at her core, a lonely, helpless feeling, an emptiness that feels older than she is, some knowledge or sadness that she can't leave behind. She doesn't say that she closes her eyes against the feeling, until there is the sound of a pickup in the driveway, the reflection of the raw sky in the mirror over the kitchen sink, the sun going down, another marker of time.

I think this is enough for now, Lennie says. Enough to start the frame, anyway. I'm cold. You?

Avery helps Lennie gather the scattered cuttings, tie them together with the twine. Lennie hands her a bundle of twigs, picks up two larger ones. They start across the scoured field, walk into clouds of their own breath, toward Lovell's barn.

Avery points into the distance, toward the old prop-erty, where fingers of bare apple trees reach into the gray sky.

I feel like a character in a Grimm's fairy tale, she says. Like we should be looking for the trail of breadcrumbs.

Lennie laughs.

In the tack room, Lennie stands the willow bundles in buckets of water.

This keeps them soft and workable, she tells Avery. Lennie then makes a web of her fingers as she describes how, once the cradle is made, the sticks will dry, and the pieces will shrink together to form a strong frame that will, she says, last forever.

june 1970

AVERY WAITS FOR her sister to breathe, to open her eyes, to make a surprised sound and sit up in the quilt-lined coffin. She wants to shake her, to yell at her to come back. She needs to touch her, but can't—can only get close enough to see that Jean Ann is wearing her Easter dress—the one that matches own.

Someone has put lipstick on Jean Ann, folded her hands over the blue satin sash. From where she stands, Avery can see that the ditch water has dried out of her hair. Someone has combed it, put in a blue plastic barrette the way Grandma Coleman does to get them ready for Sunday school.

Last night, Grandma told Avery that Jean Ann is already in Heaven. Avery pictures the streets made of gold, the happy people, maybe even Grandpa Coleman waiting for her. No more earthly pain. No more sin, Grandma said.

The grownups have come to look at Jean Ann, wearing her Easter dress, lying dead in her own living room. They fill the rooms of the house—rooms too full of light that hurts Avery's eyes, too full of the smell of strange food. They talk around Avery, over her head, as if she's not here. When they notice her, they tilt their heads, murmur, touch her hair. Poor baby, only one now. God's will.

Avery wants to be mad at God, but can't. She can't stand looking at her mother, her father, is relieved they can't see her, don't touch her like the others. She is afraid they wish she would have died instead of Jean Ann, is afraid they know everything is her fault.

She goes out onto the porch, into the light that hurts her eyes. Kids run across the yard—yelling, then whispering, yelling again. Their feet make thumping noises on the ground.

Avery sits on the porch swing, stares at her patent leather shoes. A girl in a black skirt stops running, comes to the edge of the porch, says, That your sister in there? The dead girl?

Avery nods.

The skin around the girl's eyes tightens. She tilts her head like the grownups in the house. Why isn't she at the funeral home? Your family too poor? she asks.

No! Avery blurts. She stares at the girl, feels the inside of her ears throb.

You're weird, the girl says.

Get out of here, then! Avery yells. Tears drop onto her dress.

The screendoor opens. Her father. He comes out, sits down on the swing, pulls Avery onto his lap, lets her cry. She cries into the collar of his white dress shirt, his neck, into the familiar smell of soap and sweat that mixes with her tears and snot.

The frontyard is quiet, kids gone. Grandma Coleman hands Frank a wet washcloth. He pulls Avery off his shoulder, props her with his arm, puts the cold cloth on her head. It smells of drying in air, sunlight.

She has stopped crying, can't get her breath. The cloth has wet the hair around her face, has pulled all the pain into a rectangle on her forehead, numbed it.

She lets her father carry her like a baby. He takes her into the house, into his and Madeline's bedroom, lays her on the bed. Avery hears Grandma say, Give her some of this.

The medicine comes out of the eyedropper like oil, tastes sour on her tongue. She lies down, feels her father cover her with a blanket. I'll be back to check on you, he says.

Avery feels her edges dissolving. Somewhere in the house, Grandma Coleman's voice. The sound of it comes into the room, swirls around the bed, lifts the edge of a memory of Grandma standing at the ironing board, sprinkling clothes with water, telling Avery about the sin eaters back home in West Virginia.

A long time ago, she said, the sin eater went to houses where dead people were laid out. For a little money or some eggs, coal, they ate food off plates laid on dead people's chests—eating the person's sins so they could go to Heaven.

Avery sees the old man knocking on the backdoor. He does not speak to anyone as he walks through the house—this house—in a brown coat that smells like mothballs and dust. He sits by the bed—this bed—chewing bread and stringy meat he pulls apart with long, yellow fingernails. She feels the weight of the plate on her chest.

home

AVERY DRIVES PAST the grade school, the Furnace Café, the Hi-Tide Tavern. Then, the sled hill at the edge of town—an anthill of beautiful boys, even on Christmas Eve. Finally, open country.

She crosses and recrosses the center line to avoid smears of black ice, catching swarms of crystals in her low beams, homing.

Along River Road, frost-furred branches and islands of blackberry bushes float between the bottomland and two-lane. Then, river fog, gauzy darkness that dissolves familiar fences and trees, erases the home place as she passes.

Avery can still see her breath inside the car when she makes the turn into the next driveway, follows the curve of frost-rigid gravel around the barn. She scans ahead for Davis's truck, hopes he made it home before her.

Lovell's pickup is parked by the shed, close enough that the passenger door would have banged against the scoured wood had someone opened it. Avery takes this for a sign that Lennie has gone to Warm Springs, after all, spending Christmas with her mother Bernita.

Madeline's battered Escort sits on the frozen yard to the right of the driveway—a fair job of parking. Avery wants to believe this is a sign her mother is sober. When she pulls alongside the Escort, she sees Davis's pickup parked just in front of it, outside the reach of the porch light. A spray of muddy ice on the front fender tells her the drive back from Waitsburg was rough.

Fluorescent light sifts through the plastic-covered kitchen window, lays blurry rectangles on the porch boards. Avery sits down on the cold metal settee, bends over her slight mound of belly, unzips her boots. She notices the loose strand of Christmas lights dripping off the gutter, a pool of white sparks on Mary's lavender bed. She feels the house, the whole place settle around her.

DAVIS STANDS AT the kitchen sink, draining hot water from a pot of potatoes.

I thought I heard you out there, he says.

It takes me a little longer to get my boots off now. The drive a little rough coming from Waitsburg?

Jesus, he says. I finished the last horse around noon and didn't get back to town 'til almost seven.

He motions toward the stove, says, Elk steak and mashed potatoes. Just for you. And, I found a handful of morels in the freezer.

She smiles at him, says, I finished up my Christmas shopping.

Me, too, he says, then grins. At the hardware store. And the truck stop.

She stands behind him now, watches the hair around his neck and ears curl from the steam, smells the damp flannel smell of him.

Where's Mom? she says into his shoulder.

Asleep in the back bedroom. I know what you're thinking, but I don't think she's had very much to drink today. She just said she was tired, and she went to bed.

I'll wake her up when dinner's about ready, then, Avery says.

From the living room, the sound of the tv, the recliner footrest snapping down. Lovell.

Then he is in the doorway, sock-footed, holding a beer. Thought I heard you, he says. What'd you bring me?

Lovell, Davis, Madeline—all here, she thinks—even Lennie coming back in a few days.

september 1984

DAVIS DISMOUNTS THE bay, leads him to where Avery pulls dry sunflower stalks out of the ground by the shed. He pats the horse on the neck and rump, says, Lovell said we'll surely make a horse of him—said I got a good deal on him.

He's a handsome one, she says, points to the black-socked feet. She pulls up a headless flower stalk, bangs it on the shed wall to get the dirt out of its roots, misses Mary—dead two weeks now.

She says, Who are you figuring will take care of him until you get back next summer?

You'll be here, won't you? he says, puts his hand on her arm. Were you going somewhere?

I don't—wasn't sure what would happen to the place now Mary's gone. I thought I would live in town—not with Mom, though. I'd maybe work, take some classes at the college. Lennie wants to teach me how to catch babies.

You can stay here. Mom and Dad don't want this place—aren't going to move away from Boise. Grandad always said it's better for a house to be lived in.

Avery puts her forehead to Old Man's neck, lets the tears fall. Davis circles her with his arms, turns her toward him, says into her ear, Stay here. Go to school—do all those things you want. I'll come back when I'm through with farrier school, live with you.

august 1970

ALL NIGHT, THE opening and closing of the screendoor, murmurs in Madeline's kitchen, reflection of headlights sweeping across the dresser mirror that woke Avery several times. Now, grainy daylight, explosions of pink Kleenex on the dull living room floor, Madeline curled on the green couch, asleep, wearing the same clothes she wore the day before. Still here—not like Frank, gone since yesterday morning when he stepped off the porch carrying his work lunch, walked off toward the grain elevator, disappeared into the wheatfield.

It is Mary that Avery finds in the kitchen, Mary who has stayed all night again, the same as when Jean Ann died a few weeks ago—Mary who tries to explain.

Sweetie, I believe your daddy is fine, she says. He just needed to go away for a while. He's sad about Jean Ann. He'll be back, he'll be back.

Avery stares at the pan of biscuits on the table. Too orange on top—from a can—not the kind Mary makes at home. A metal taste rises in her mouth. She looks away—at the stove, the floor, pictures her father's black socks, his boots under the smoldering heap of soft work shirt, dark blue pants—a pile of clothes singeing the wheat.

Her father is gone, she knows, snatched up by God— gone to be with Jean Ann. He isn't coming back, is lost to the Rapture Avery has heard Grandma Coleman talk about.

january 1980

THEY LIE IN sleeping bags on top of saddle blankets in the back of Lovell's pickup, looking into the smear of Milky Way above them. Avery turns to Lennie, says, How's Mr. Carr even gonna know if we actually see this thing?

Don't know, Lennie says. Honor system, I guess. She raises up on an elbow, puts the wine bottle to her lips. Damn, it's cold out here.

Avery takes the bottle from her, takes a long drink, sets the bottle back in the corner of the pickup bed. When she lies down, she feels the sky pull back a bit.

Mr. Carr says we have almost ten thousand miles of blood vessels in our bodies, she says. Right now, I can feel that wine rolling through every one of them.

Oh, Lord, Lennie says. Take it easy, Avery. We have school tomorrow.

No, Avery says, then, I know. Listen. Think about all those blood vessels inside us. All those stars out there, she says, lifts her chin toward the sky.

Lennie's voice is louder now. You ever think about how the light from those stars is so old—how those things are probably not even there anymore? Makes me feel like this life is just a flash—all of this happens in an eyeblink.

Avery says, Yeah. I was thinking today, even if we do get to see this comet tonight, we probably won't be alive the next time it comes around.

Lennie sits up, reaches across Avery, giggles, says, Then this is our one big chance for extra credit, so reach me that bottle.

Avery keeps talking to the sky. When I was little— before—I used to think Mom and Dad, Jean Ann—all of us were dolls. That our house was really just a dollhouse.

She can hear Lennie gulping the wine.

This whole place—everything—the trees, pastures, phone poles—weren't actually real—that everything we did was only because whoever was playing with the doll-house was making it happen. We were just a part of a story. Maybe not even real.

Lennie says, I used to think that our radio had little people in it, that they just sat in there on little chairs, wearing little cowboy hats and neck scarves, or dresses with sequins, and waited for us to turn on the radio so they could sing.

Avery smiles, says, You ever see *The Twilight Zone*? Mom and Dad used to watch that sometimes after Jean Ann and me went to bed. Once, I can't remember why, I got to stay up to watch it.

Avery hears Lennie swallow again, feels her staring at the side of her face.

You ever see the one where the people thought they were normal until they found out they were really living in a fake toy town where some giant kid was playing, moving stuff around to make everything happen? I think that must be where I got the idea. Anyway, everything looks normal until this huge kid peeks over the edge of the scene, then reaches his big hand in. That scared the bejeezus out of me—those people's faces when they found out. Only difference was, I made up a story for us where nothing bad could happen.

Avery stops talking, registers that she is drunk, that her mother is not home—hasn't been there in two days.

Can I go home with you? she asks. I can't go to Paul and Mary's, drunk like this.

What do you think? Lennie says.

An airplane blinks red in the sky.

I think we've missed the comet, Avery says.

Damn. Probably because you were talking so much, Lennie says.

Avery rolls toward Lennie, says, Probably because we're drunk.

november 1970

PAUL'S WOODEN LEG is propped against the end table. Avery sets his slice of apple pie on the table, tries to not stare at the pinned and doubled-over leg of his pants.

Thank you, Little Bit. You make that pie? he grins.

No sir, she says, not realizing he's teasing. But I did carry the apple peels out when Mary was finished peeling.

Back in the kitchen, she measures, stirs two spoons of sugar into the cup of the coffee Mary has poured for Paul. She pokes a fork through the clogged holes in the lid of the evaporated milk can, as Mary has shown her, counts to three, measuring a thin stream of the milk into the coffee.

Paul takes the cup from her, looks into it. Just right, he says. Just right.

He sips the coffee, nods toward the leg. Had to take it off. That thing was makin' me sore.

Avery touches the leather strap, asks, How does it stay on?

He sets the coffee on the table, picks up the dish. I'll show you sometime. He wags one of his caterpillar eyebrows, then he points the pie fork toward the tv, says, News is comin' on.

Mary is washing dishes. Steam, lemon smell rising out of the sink. She rinses her hands, holds out a dish towel. Here, she says. Dry the silverware for me.

Avery drags a chair over to the drainboard, kneels on its seat, wipes at the mismatched forks and spoons, the paring knife.

That knife's old, Mary tells her. I brought that out to Oregon with me. It was Mommy's. She said I'd need it to peel all those apples we was going to grow. She was right.

Avery runs her thumb over the smooth wooden handle, traces the oily grooves of letters carved into it.

Old Hickory, Mary's saying. The best there is.

PAUL IS ASLEEP, head thrown back, mouth slack, open. Mary turns down the tv, motions toward her green recliner, says, Come over here. Sit down by me.

Avery sits down on the edge of the seat cushion. Mary pulls her into her lap, onto the thick legs beneath the dress she wears. Avery can smell the coffee on her breath.

Mary shifts her hips. Don't sit so big, she says. Then, her voice goes low. You're a wonderin' about Paul's leg? Well, I'm just going to tell you and get it over with so you won't have to wonder any more.

Avery's cheeks burn. She wants to get off Mary's lap, go to the back bedroom to read, draw.

Mary points at Paul's empty pant leg. He lost that leg in the mines. A big timber fell on it, and he couldn't work no more, which is the reason we came here, just about six months after your granny and grandpa did.

may 1982

H E PULLS HIS fists to his chest, points one elbow at the ground, one at the sky. His arms become wings, he hops on his right foot, lifts his left knee off the ground, switches, dips. The horsehair fringes hanging from his waist, the arms of his outfit move like grass in the wind.

Lennie ignores the other dancers whirling around the arena—does not take her eyes from him. Wesley Rideout, she says to Avery. Nez Perce. No kin that I know of.

He crouches, stretches his right foot away from his body, bounces on the pivot of his left foot.

Looks like a lawn sprinkler, Avery says, grinning.

Lennie tries to frown, but smiles instead, says, At the end of this round, there'll be an Owl Dance. Hide and watch whether I don't ask him to dance.

Don't doubt you will, Avery says.

I'm going to marry him, Lennie says. Soon as I go off over to Warm Springs and learn how to deliver babies, I'm going to come back and marry Wes Rideout.

I don't doubt that, either, Avery says. I'm going on home. Davis should be there by now.

At the car, she turns, looks back toward the arbor, sees Lennie, still there, at the edge, watching, lit up by afternoon sun. She bounces her knees to the beat of the drum, throwing sparks off the black flint of her hair.

AT HOME, AVERY finds Davis's pickup is in the driveway. In the kitchen, Mary sets a plate of sliced tomatoes on the dinner table, says, He got here about noon. Paul's already had him working, then she nods toward the kitchen door. I think he's out there in the bunkhouse—resting.

The heavy oak door is open. He is lying across the bed with his arm across his face. She knocks on the doorjamb, wishes she'd given herself more time to study him.

He sits up, tugs at his open shirtfront.

Hi, he says. Thought I heard you drive up.

She can smell him from the door: the scent of sweat and dust in the cotton cloth of his shirt, like the smell of every man she loved—Lovell, Paul, her father—but somehow magnified.

He sets his work boots on the floor, stares at her, grins. Dust motes swarm the blade of light slicing the air between them.

How was the powwow? he asks.

Fun, she says. Lennie's in love with a grass dancer from Lapwai—full Nez Perce.

He stands up, buttons his shirt. She waits, doesn't move, is afraid he will walk past her, but he stops, kisses her. Then again, and all the way to the house, she can feel the heat of him behind her.

august 1970

AUNT VELVIE'S YARD, house, kitchen, are full of wet heat that Avery isn't used to—West Virginia heat that presses against her cheeks and forehead, anchors her to the kitchen chair. It prickles the hair on her arms, makes her sleepy—makes Grandma's and Aunt Velvie's shoes stick to the linoleum. She pictures reaching out to squeeze the air like a sponge, imagines drops of water falling when she does. Dog days, Grandma calls it.

The blackberries they picked this morning over on Lick Branch simmer on the stove, bite the air with their smell, bruise spoons and countertops.

Grandma lifts a canning jar from a pot of boiling water with tongs, says, Avery, go on out on the porch. I'll call you in when the burries are done, saying *berries* the way Aunt Velvie does. You can help set the lids on the jars.

On the porch, less heat, but the day still heavy, still a strong current that slows Avery's movement. She lies on the swing, hangs one leg over the side, closes her eyes. Petunias, burnt-cloth smell from the knotted rag in the coffee can on the porch rail—Uncle Cleve's gnat smoke.

Laughter in the kitchen, Grandma saying, I thought Daddy would wring his neck! Then more laughter swirling in Avery's ears, boring into her chest, making her furious. She wants to run back into the house and scream, Don't laugh! Jean Ann is dead! Daddy is gone!

She sits up, braces her feet on the porch boards, pushes off. Hard. The swing wobbles, the chain creaks near the hook in the ceiling. She pushes again, lies down, sinks, lets the heat close around her.

hole

SWATH OF LIGHT finds an opening in the gray flannel sky, spins the stand of willows into threads of honey. At the edge of the pond, Avery cuts twigs with pruners and lays them in a pile. Her belly has changed into a convex lens through which she sees everything, that makes bending over hard for her. Before she picks up the bundle, her arms already know its weight. Her hands already feel the curve of fiber, know the shape of the chair.

She makes a clean cut at the base of a thick shoot, and something—a whiff of pond mud or the raw smell coming from the wounded twig—rises up and releases a dream that clinches her lungs, makes her stand upright, staring into a middle distance that she doesn't see.

WINDY DAY—SOMETIME between winter and spring. Clouds and sun. Warm, then cold, then warm again. It's sometime after Easter because she is wearing the sweater with the kittens on it that went with her Easter dress.

In Room 11, her mother is passed out on the bed, her right hand made into a fist. A shining filament of drool falls out of her open mouth, makes a dark pool on the bedspread.

Outside, Avery stands at the edge of the parking lot and tries to recognize shapes of letters in shards of glass. There is a straight red line that could be an *l* or an *i*, maybe part of a *w*. When she looks up, she sees mountains in the distance, but doesn't recognize their shapes, either.

She does not know the name of the place she is— where the man dropped them off early this morning and paid for the room—does not know the name of the motel, because a windstorm has shattered the sign into this pile of glass.

She finds the hole behind the motel. A big tree is lying near it. *Wind.* She has never seen this before. Never a tree lying down and never the roots with dirt and rocks stuck between them.

Her snow boots land soft. Down inside the hole, the ground is just higher than her knees. She can see the line of light brown dirt near where the grass grows—the same color as the dirt in the roots of the tree—and then the coffee color of the dirt that goes all the way deep down below where she is.

Avery lies down in the hole, out of the wind, but she feels the coldness of dirt against her legs and the back of her Easter sweater. There is an old smell, like a root cellar, like a grave. She is going to be in trouble, but this is what her mother gets for leaving her alone, she thinks.

Above her, sky like a blue bedsheet on a clothesline. She looks at it so long she feels she will fall against it.

She crosses her arms on her chest, remembers what a girl at church told her—that dead people's fingernails and hair don't stop growing. She pictures her own hair piling up around her, her nails growing into the coffee-colored dirt.

Back in Room 11, the air conditioner shudders. There are marks on the side of Madeline's face from the bedspread. Now, the fist is gone and now, the smell on her breath isn't beer. It's the smell of someplace far away, where Avery can't go. It's the smell of a place with all of the light gone out of it.

august 1970

AVERY WAVES BACK at the Grange lady who brought them to the station, watches her through the train window, pretends it is the sidewalk moving instead of the train—pretends it is the lady, not her, who is going to West Virginia. Then, the lady and the station vanish into the darkness.

Beside her, Grandma Coleman rests her head against the seat, eyes closed, knotty fingers spread across the black cover of the Bible in her lap—the Bible that holds all those stories.

Avery closes her own eyes, feels the slow curve of the track, thinks of home, of her mother left behind them, of Lot's wife in Grandma's Bible. She squeezes her eyes tighter, tries to not look back. She thinks, *Pillow of salt*. Pillow of salt, she whispers.

Then, the train is moving faster, taking them east. Avery watches darkness sweep past the reflection of her own face in the glass, feels her edges dissolve, herself float up into the noise that is everywhere at once.

The train curves around the edge of a hill. Through the window across the aisle, the lights of town spill down hillsides, pile along streets like diamonds. Avery thinks of her mother. Tonight Madeline *is* one of those lights on Main Street—the brightest, the one that will burn until morning.

NIGHT AGAIN. SMALL towns flashing by. Avery fogs the window with her breath, tries to write her name. Grandma's face hovers behind her in the window—a ghost. Quit that, she says.

AFTERNOON SUN BURNS the sky white above the mountains, the frothing trees, the houses that nudge the tracks—thickens the air inside the train. Grandma worries the cover of her Bible, reads small white signs that name the towns they pass: Belle, Glasgow, Boomer.

Above the falls at Glen Ferris, the Gauley River is wide, flat, green, then it thins, turns muddy brown. Giant, sand-colored rocks sit in it like molars.

At Cotton Hill Station, the train slows, stops. Avery follows Grandma down the aisle, the stairs. She steps out into the smells of diesel and river, into the arms and faces that press in, grab her, squeeze her, smell like soap and talcum.

THE CAR CLIMBS, bores into the cool tunnel of trees. Avery sits close to Grandma on the back seat, tries to remember the names of the man, the woman, listens to their round-edged words.

She wakes when the car stops. Night, a big white house, hundreds of flickering green lights in the air, on the trees and lawn. Lightning bugs, the man says. He lifts the trunk lid, takes out suitcases. Avery stands in the yard, watching stems of grass ignite around her.

ruby

THE DOG IS draped over the shoulder of the road like a coat tossed from a passing car. A corner of the red bandana around its neck lifts in the wind as they pass it. Lovell stops. A whirring sound from under the pickup as he backs up.

Is it dead? Avery asks.

Don't know yet. Be right back.

He opens the truck door, steps out. Avery doesn't wait, follows him toward the brindled dog.

Red heeler, he says.

The dog's eyes are open, its ribs heave.

Stand back, Lovell says. Sometimes they'll bite when they're hurt.

He squats, scoops up the dog, says, Good girl. It's OK.

Avery follows him back to the truck, opens the tailgate, shoves a feed bucket toward the cab. The dog makes a faint whine when Lovell lays her in the truck bed.

I'm taking her to the vet, he says.

Avery brushes her hand across the dog's stiff hair. I'll ride in back.

Nope, he says, points at her belly. That wouldn't be right. Nothin' you can do, anyway. She'll either live or die.

Live, Avery says. She pets the dog again. Ruby, she says.

flight

AVERY'S ARMS FEEL heavy. She lays the magazine on her chest, closes her eyes, thinks of Mary in this house, this room, pregnant with Caroline all those years ago. Her thoughts move forward twenty years to Caroline, herself, pregnant with Davis.

Near sleep, Avery registers the sound of small thuds coming from the living room—a sound like a moth hurling itself into a lamp bulb. It's afternoon, and she hasn't yet put on the lights.

She is alone—Davis and Lovell gone to town. She knows she ought to get up and find out what is making the noise, but she can't make herself do it.

She rolls to her side. Her belly curves outward from her body, pulling her spine inward. She is carrying the baby low, can almost hear Grandma Coleman say, That low, it will surely be a boy.

It's now difficult for her to lift or bend, still, she spent this morning filling troughs, raking leaves that blew against fences during the winter, then had to stay inside the house to rest after lunch.

Most days, Avery waits until afternoon to lie down when the sunlight falls through the bedroom window, pooling on the bedspread, to lie down in its warmth and drift, to breathe through the Braxton Hicks contractions that cinch her belly—the uneven spasms Lennie calls "practice runs." She lies in the only comfortable position she can find for her new body: on her left side with her right knee drawn up as if she is about to take a step.

Sometimes, while she rests, the baby rests, as well, a warm, low flame within her.

At other times, it stirs and sparks against the dark walls of her belly. Elbows and heels arc across her abdomen, keep her awake, press against her bladder, until she finally gets up and goes to the bathroom, then usually, the baby will quiet down again. Avery will doze, holding the tiny live coal inside the cave of her body until the sunlight has moved across the bed and then the room, and the chill air falls over her.

Now, thuds from the living room. Avery pushes herself up onto an elbow, then a hand, swings her legs over the edge of the bed. She stops in the hallway, short of the front room, listens to the small impacts against glass. A trapped bee, a loose branch, tapping fingertips?

She moves closer so she can see across the room. There is a movement high on the inside of the picture window, a flare of red, a tiny body battering the glass. Hummingbird.

As a child, she had tried to catch the hummingbirds that worried the petunias in the wheelbarrows and tire planters in Grandma Coleman's yard, until her grandma said, Stop it. It can't be done. No human has ever touched a hummingbird. Avery believed her. She stopped trying. Instead, she just watched, tried to picture the shape, the exact color of the hammering wings.

Now, a hummingbird inside her house—a whirring bundle of hollow bone and heart, held up by invisible wings, throwing itself over and over against the glass. She crosses the room, opens the front door wide, backs up, waits. Still, feather and glass.

Avery moves to the window, puts up her hands, forms a cup around the bird. It feels like a small, warm breath.

She steps into the doorway and opens her hands. The bundle lifts a few feet, levitates, flies around the side of the house. She looks at her palms, half expecting a spray of the luminous dust of butterflies and moths.

september 1971

AVERY ARROWS HER right tennis shoe, pokes the empty potato chip bag on the floorboard. Cooling engine tick. One Mississippi, two Mississippi, she whispers. The ticks come too far apart now to count.

She stares at the tavern door, at the small window near the top, the brick of light it throws onto the gravel—tries to stare hard enough to cause her mother to come through that door to take her home.

The door opens. Music, more light, man in a white cowboy shirt. Avery hears his steps, the gravel kicking off the toes of his boots. As he passes the car, he bends down, looks at her through the door window, shakes his head. He crosses the parking lot, the alley. From the darkness, he yells, Let 'er buck, goddammit!

Avery unfolds the blanket her mother left on the backseat, the one she took from the closet before they left home earlier today. It smells like their house, their house before everything changed. She arrows each foot, pries off the opposite shoe, lies down under the blanket, listening. She runs her fingers over the hard ridges of the steering wheel, touches the cold metal horn. Shev-ro-let, shev-ro-let, she says to herself.

A SOUND LIKE tiny bells brings her out of the shell of sleep the blanket has molded around her, opens her eyes. She pushes herself up with a tingling arm, turns toward the sound—toward her mother's face on the other side of the window.

Madeline leans against the door, stabs at it with her car keys. Avery pulls up the lock.

Move over, Madeline says through the window glass. She jerks open the door, grabs the steering wheel, hauls herself into the car, slams the door, leans forward, lays her forehead on the wheel. OK, she says. OK.

Avery waits. There is only the sound of her mother's breath and the ripe apple smell of it that begins to fill the car.

A pickup shoots through the alley, honking its horn. Madeline's head jerks up. Now, she mumbles. Right now.

Avery watches the slow motion movie of her mother tipping, sliding toward her. Then, her mother's head lands on her, the weight of her head pinning her own legs to the seat.

The sky is starting to fade at the edges. People come out of the tavern, starting their motors, driving away.

Avery leans down, lifts a stand of her mother's hair, brings it to her nose. Reek of cigarettes. She lifts the collar of Madeline's blouse. A smell like the mint fields over at La Grande, some man's aftershave. She shifts her hips, pulls a corner of the blanket off the floorboard, rubs the satin edge of it.

When she wakes again, the sky has turned the color of a salmon's belly, the tops of the mountains dark against it. She is cold except where Madeline's head is damp and heavy on her tingling legs.

She needs to pee, doesn't want to miss school today. One Mississippi, she begins.

vessels

AVERY STANDS IN the yard just outside the shade line of the house, gathering sun, practicing the breathing Lennie has taught her. It's still, the air unmoving—a day between seasons. The air she draws deep into her chest has lost the dampness of spring, but the sky has not yet gone to the thin milk color of summer.

For days, she has waited for the sudden energy Lennie has told her will come before labor. She walks across the yard, pushing her arms and legs through thick water.

On a nail in the shed, a stoneware cup the color of a robin's egg. Avery stretches up on her toes and lifts it, looks inside. It's been out there awhile. Brown flakes of dried coffee cover the bottom.

She has learned to read the bottoms of the cups and mugs scattered over the place like reading tea leaves, but instead of predicting the future, the cups tell her stories of what's already been. The white ceramic mug on the picnic table with the puddle of ants in it—Lovell's, he takes sugar. Brown flakes curled in the bottom say Davis, coffee black.

She pokes around in the pickup beds and floorboards, then checks the back porch: one thermos, two plastic glasses—no ants, probably unsweetened tea—and five cups. She carries them into the house and drops all but the thermos into a pan of hot dishwater.

Davis leans into Arlee's flank, bent on the hinge of his hips, holding one of Arlee's legs between his knees. The thin cotton shirt he wears is soaked through, translucent against the bay of Arlee's hindquarter. He taps in a last nail, sets down the foot, turns to pat Arlee's flank. Dust flies up from under his hand.

When he sees Avery, he grins.

Hey there. It's a question.

I'm fine, she tells him.

He pulls off his cap and wipes a sleeve across his forehead. His hair has gone wavy and dark with sweat.

Almost done here. I have to run over to McCrae's and shoe his paint mare after this. You want to ride over?

I thought I might take a nap, Avery says. Baby's quiet today.

Not much longer, eh? Aren't you glad you're not a horse?

Avery knows he meant it for a joke, but she feels irritation push into her neck and arms like stiff bristles. She smiles then shrugs.

Davis puts down the hammer and moves toward her.

She presses her face against his chest. He inhales, lays a palm against the back of her head. Her hair instantly goes damp under it.

You smell like sweat and fly dope, she says into his shirt.

Thanks, he says. You sure you don't want to go with? Maybe the ride will get you started.

Nope. I'm fine here. Just tired. Besides, I can't have this baby until Mom comes back from wherever she's gone to.

Davis unties Arlee from the corral post. I won't be gone long.

Avery points at the coffee cup on the toolbox, a match for the one in the shed, and waits. He picks it up and hands it to her. He grins.

You're going in, anyway, he says.

The dishwater has gone cold, so Avery runs hot water into the pan. Her face damp with steam and her belly pushed against the rim of the counter. She stands as close as she can, but still, she has to lean over a bit to reach the sink.

She feels her hands swell as she fumbles for the cups and glasses in the bottom of the dishpan. When she's washed and rinsed them all, she rinses the thermos and takes up a dish towel. When she lifts her arms to put a mug into the cabinet, she feels the give between her legs, the warm rivulet on her thigh, then calf and ankle.

She looks down at the clear water pooling beneath her bare instep. It does not stop.

birth

LENNIE'S FACE HOVERS over Avery's, telling her to breathe. Don't forget to breathe.

Avery hears Lennie breathe for her, sees the smeared outline of Davis's face beside the bed, then feels his hand in her hair. She moves away from it.

All afternoon, the contractions built, each one sending a gush of warmth from Avery, soaking the pads she wore between her legs as she walked around the house and yard. The water had a sweet, clean smell to it, like the sugar water Paul had boiled up to feed orphaned calves.

Avery, I'm going to check you after this contraction, she hears Lennie say.

There is the pressure of Lennie's hand inside her, then Avery feels Lennie step back, feels the first clot pass out of her. She opens her eyes. The overhead light is on now. Davis is standing near the foot of the bed. She hears him say *blood*.

Lennie's right hand is suspended in the air. Blood drips from it.

Avery tries to sit up, sees the streaks of red leaching toward the edges of the pad, hears Lennie enunciate *9-1-1*, feels someone ease her back onto the mattress.

She is lightheaded. The water closes over her, and she is at the bottom of a river, everything around her slow and silt-hazed. She hears the rush of time above her, the voices in the room moving faster than she can listen. It is dark where she is, and still. Pressure on her eardrums. Then, the next contraction jerks her upward into the light and noise. She is blind, ready to explode.

august 1972

AVERY CAN SMELL the bay horse from where she stands, his sweaty smell, something underneath—terror, desire.

Lovell tightens the cinch, pulls the stirrup off the saddle seat, lets it drop against Arlee's side.

I named this ol' boy after the town where Lennie's mom was born. Had him for about seven year. Still rides good.

He puts the bit in Arlee's mouth. He'll take good care of you, he says.

Avery feels the hinges of her knees give, leans against the gate. The metal taste of fear in her mouth, memory of another hot, brittle day.

MILKY SKY, BLUNT pain in the back of her head. Her father standing over her, the sun a halo behind him. He pulls her to her feet, lifts her hair, looks under it, says, You're not hurt.

Tears scald her cheeks. Madeline laughs, says to Frank, You better put her right back on or she won't ever do it again.

Avery shaking her head, sobbing, watching her father walk toward the pony that drags its reins through the apple orchard.

COME HERE, LOVELL says. He squats, makes a cup with his hands, holds it below the stirrup. Put your foot in here, he says. She wobbles toward him, hesitates when Arlee shifts his feet. The metal taste moves further across her tongue.

It's alright. C'mon, he says. Lennie rides him, he adds.

Avery steps into Lovell's hands. Grab the saddle horn, he tells her. She feels him lift her, hears him grunt, then Arlee is beneath her—solid and alive, moving sideways, making her claw at the saddle horn.

Whoa. Good boy, Lovell says, puts his hand on the side of Arlee's neck. He smoothes it toward the saddle, hands Avery the reins. Hold these loose, your elbows out, he says, then taps the saddle horn with his scarred finger. Don't let those reins fall behind this horn.

Lovell takes the lead rope, starts toward the pasture gate, Avery feeling Arlee's weight shift, the movements that begin as sparks deep in his bones before they ignite, rise through muscle and skin, burn into her legs.

Already, the reins are wet from her hands, and the horse smell stronger in her throat and nose. She keeps her eyes on Lovell, trying not to grab the saddle horn, trying to breathe.

surfacing

AVERY.

She hears the voice, swims up toward it. Rough fingertips wipe at her cheek. Davis. She opens her eyes, and there he is, his face the color of Styrofoam. He has been crying.

There is burning pain—between her hip bones, she thinks—a dull roar behind her eyelids as she tries to hold them open. Her teeth click together. Mom, she says.

She has no idea how much time has passed since she was last awake, since she pushed her baby into the wide silence of the room then felt the weight of him on her chest, a watery glimpse of fine, dark hair pasted to his head, the blue of his skin like thin milk.

Pain, she says and slips under again, beneath the hiss and whir of machines, drifting away from the nurse's voice, the metal drag of a curtain across a rod. She does not want to go back toward the voices, toward Davis's hand just now on her face.

perfect

THE NURSE LAYS him in Avery's arms, nods at Davis, says, Take as long as you need. Call me when you're ready. She sets a pair of tiny scissors on the bed tray and leaves.

Avery unfolds the receiving blanket he's wrapped in, lets it fall across the bedsheet, across her knees like blue petals. And there is the full length of him. She hears Davis draw a deep breath.

A mat of fuzz covers the baby's face. His lips are soft, parted a little, still moist. Avery kisses them, inhales.

His hair has dried to the color of corn silk. Fine sprigs stick out from his round head. She smoothes it, looks at Davis, whispers, Your hair.

Davis lays a finger inside the baby's palm, which is cupped as if it has been dipping water, then he runs it up and down the length of the tiny arm. Perfect, he says.

Lennie brings in a basin and cloth. With the scissors the nurse left, she helps Davis cut a lock of his hair and curls it into a small envelope. She helps Avery ink the soles of his tiny feet then transfers the footprints to a sheet of white paper, then squeezes Davis's arm and sits down in the vinyl chair by the bed.

Davis opens the plastic bag he holds, pulls out the baby's outfit he's brought from home. He lays it on the tray, then stands beside Avery.

Together, Avery and Davis wash their child. Davis holds him over the basin while Avery brushes a soft, damp washcloth over his skin. They powder him, diaper and dress him in the green flannel gown, then wrap him in a blanket Bernita has sent.

Davis cradles the baby to his chest, his battered fingers spread across the blanket. He sits down on the edge of the bed, says, We need to name him.

His voice is low, and it cracks a little.

Jackson Russell, like we said before, Avery says.

Alright then, he says.

After they are gone, and the room is quiet, Avery touches her belly. Through the gown, she gathers slack flesh between her fingers, pushes into the valleys of skin, trying to find the familiar hardness of the baby.

She touches a breast. Needle pricks just below the skin and a rush of heaviness toward the nipple. She feels the wetness on the cotton gown, thinks of her mother nursing Jean Ann.

The first sound comes from someplace outside her, slamming against her throat, pushing through her skin. It burrows deeper inside her, grabs her breath, pushes its way back out.

Now, a nurse stands by the bed, her hand burning Avery's shoulder. Aw, honey, she says. Somebody forgot—we'll give you a shot for that.

She tugs at the gown tie behind Avery's neck. Let's get you cleaned up.

Avery cannot speak. She cannot make the words to tell this.

lennie explains

ENNIE STANDS BY the bed, rubbing the back of Avery's hand with her thumb. It was nothing you did, she says, repeating what the on-call doctor had told Avery and Davis a few hours ago. The placenta detached and there wasn't a thing you could have done to prevent that. Everything looked fine up until you started bleeding.

Avery closes her eyes. Tears. She pulls her hand away from Lennie's.

I don't want to be here, she says.

I know, Lennie says. But, you lost a lot of blood. We could've lost you.

Avery turns her face to the window, opens her eyes.

I don't want to go home, either, she whispers. I don't think I can stand it.

lilacs

T HE DAY IS a bridge between wet spring and unfolding summer. The sun, nearly straight overhead, shoots hard light through gaps in the thick
clouds. Blades of cold wind sweep across the fields, leaving the scent of ice.

Along the river, cottonwoods leaf out in a shade of
green so pure it makes Avery's eyes ache. All around her,
everything speaks above the silence inside Madeline's car
while she waits for Davis to open the door.

As Davis takes her hand to help her from the car,
Avery looks up, putting her eyes anywhere but on her
mother or Davis or the line of men already starting up
the hillside. A red-tailed hawk, probably the same one
she saw on a fence post out by the lane, banks and turns
a wide circle over the foot of the hill. She supposes it is

waiting to capture small creatures disturbed by all the movement of people and cars, and she hates the hawk for that.

Avery stands. The wind scrapes at her bare legs, making them the only part of her body she can truly feel, except for a spot somewhere between her throat and her navel that she cannot name or exactly locate that aches and aches.

Madeline comes around to where Avery and Davis stand, carrying a blanket that she keeps in the car, an old habit from the nights she slept off the liquor in the tavern parking lot before driving home. She holds it out to Avery.

Here, put this around you. I wished you'd have worn pants. Nobody would've cared if you wore pants.

Avery shakes her head and turns to look at Davis. Around them, the soft closing of car doors. Let's go, she says.

The small white casket under Lovell's arm shines bright against his dark jacket and the deep green of the new grass. He rests his right hand on its lid. He keeps his eyes down, picks his way through the rocks and mud.

Avery watches the casket as Davis leads her up the hill. She no longer feels the chill air, does not think of the mud that spills over into the flats she wears on her feet.

At the top of the hill, Avery leans against Davis, stares into the small grave that Lovell has dug, at the roots of grass made visible by the slice of their shovel blades, and even though she knows it makes no sense, she thinks of growing things, of Mary's iris bulbs that she, newly pregnant, dug and separated last fall. She thinks of the lilac bushes that have stood over other graves for years, and for a quivering moment, wishes that the tiny flowers had already pushed through the hard buds and bloomed, giving this place more color than this aching green it now is.

Lovell places the casket on two-by-fours lying across the open grave, setting it down so tenderly that it makes the ache in Avery's chest stir. Tendrils weave through her rib cage, reach down into her belly, echo of the ache in her breasts the day the baby was born. She feels Davis's arm tighten, and she leans further into him.

Pastor Jeske's words flail in the wind. Suffer the little children . . .

Avery looks across at Lennie, who wears sunglasses, then at Lovell again. His eyes are visible, and they glisten in the harsh light. He stands straight, holding his good Stetson in both hands, his arms crossed in front of him. The wind tears at long strands of hair around his collar.

Then, the casket again. Heads bow all around her, but Avery keeps her head up, her eyes on the tiny white boat run aground on the reef of boards across the grave.

Pastor Jeske's voice slows, ending his prayer. Lovell and Wes step forward to join the funeral director at the grave, then Avery feels Davis move, too. Each man takes an end of a rope and lifts the casket. Pastor draws the boards from beneath it, sets them aside.

For a moment, the casket levitates above the hole, suspended between earth and sky. Avery does not breathe. She finds the lilac bushes and holds them in her line of vision. There are no voices, no sound of wind, just the bushes with all that green and the straining buds saying to her, Not yet. Not yet.

She walks forward, lays the flowers on the casket, stands there, empty, until Lennie takes her arm and leads her back to her place. When she looks at the hole again, the casket is at the bottom. Davis takes up the shovel, then plunges it into the dirt pile, exposing the damp, dark layer of earth inside.

seeds

ALL NIGHT, THE penned-up calves bawled for their mothers. Avery is groggy. She throws her toast into the trash, thinks, *This is not the body of Christ, but the stale crust of days, the same crumbling edges of weeks after Jean Ann died, after Frank left.*

Inside the deep cave of the mailbox, her fingers slide over the slick cover of a magazine, bump against the edges of envelopes. She pulls the mail out of the box, registers the slice of paper across a fingertip.

Sun glints off the magazine cover. *Western Horseman.* Atop it, two white envelopes, one of them thick and square. Another sympathy card. There is a smear of blood across the address, already dry. She sticks the unopened card inside the magazine, waits for a car to pass before walking into a backwash of dust and hot air.

Gate, shed, barn, house. She walks past, climbs the porch stairs, sits on the glider.

She pictures herself dragging the garden hose across the yard to water the dog roses that stand along the fence, but doesn't move.

A wall of dust slams into the bedsheets on the line. This morning, Davis stripped them from the bed, washed the smell of Avery's sleep from them and hung them in the sun.

Let those hang until I get home, he'd said. *An excuse,* Avery thinks. *A way to keep me out of bed today.*

Inside the house, the telephone rings. It stops, then begins again. Lennie. Avery knows that if she doesn't answer, Lennie will drive over to check on her, but she can't get up.

On the willow table by the glider, a pile of seed packets Avery ordered from catalogs that started coming after Christmas, a yearly ritual she learned from Mary. She sifts through the envelopes, feels the hard shapes inside the paper, hears their small stirrings, hears Mary's voice, a litany of seeds: early summer squash, Kentucky Wonder, shoepeg corn.

She rips the top off a packet, pours lettuce seeds into her hand. She stands and tosses them off the porch. Some of them stick to her damp palm.

She scoops up the rest of the packets, takes them to the edge of the yard. Again and again, she flings them away from her body. They fly out of her hand and vanish into the dirt of the driveway.

Avery drops the empty packets into the burn barrel, checks the sheets on the line. She scrunches the dry fabric in her hand, lifts it, smells the dust and air that have passed through it.

Tree, stairs, door. Inside the house, it is cool. She hears a rustling and turns to look back through the screen. A wave of quail is breaking over the yard, gathering seeds. When Lennie's car comes around the shed, the birds scatter and lift.

rain

LAST NIGHT, AVERY dreamed of rain. The sound of it soaked the thin layer of her sleep. In the dream, she stood inside the back door and felt cool air swirl up her legs, move through her clothes. She pushed and pushed on the door to get out, but it wouldn't open.

Avery wakes, listens to the sound of Davis's sleep, listens to the stillness of the house.

Nights after her father left, she would lie in bed listening to silence push at the walls and ceilings, listening to the whoosh of it in her ears, knowing that her mother could hear it, too. Finally, the house expanded in the darkness, grew large enough to hold the silence that settled in and stayed long into daylight.

Before it was only Avery and her mother that were left, soft sounds had washed through the rooms—Madeline's murmuring voice, Frank's soft snores, and from the other side of the bed, Jean Ann's breath like waves across the pillowcase.

After, when she was alone in the double bed and her mother asleep somewhere else in the house—a chair, the couch, the porch swing, and always a smudged tumbler nearby—Avery slept facing Jean Ann's side of the bed. She closed her eyes and hoped that when she opened them Jean Ann would be there again. Sometimes, she put her hand into the cool space between the blanket and the sheet and left it there until the sheet warmed. Sometimes, she whispered I'm sorry into the dark cave of the house.

Now, light seeps through the summer curtains. Davis's breathing shifts. He turns over. She can feel the heat of him against her back. He stretches his legs, makes a low groan, presses his knees into the backs of hers.

Good morning, he says.

Morning.

He traces a finger down her forearm, shifts, pushes himself closer to her. She feels him lift her hair and twist it away from her neck. Damp breath. A dull ache starts up in her belly.

It's OK now, isn't it? To do this?

She hears herself say, Yes.

His hand moves to her breast. A long time, he says.

His hands travel her body, leave traces of damp-ness on the cotton gown. She registers the press of him against her, but cannot turn to him like before.

His hands stop. OK? he asks.

Her throat fills. She can't speak.

He tugs her arm, rolls her to face him. Avery?

Tears burn the rims of her eyes. It's OK, she says.

december 1971

THE INSIDE OF the car is cold, with the kind of chill Avery knows comes in the late of summer nights and stays awhile after the sun comes up— like the cool breath that rises up from creek banks on West Virginia summer evenings. And there is the sound of Madeline's sleep and the wheel grease and cigarette smell of the man beside her on the backseat. The loud sounds he makes through his nose and mouth come over the seat, wake Avery.

The backporch light over the tavern door flickers out, and Avery can see stars through the frame of the windshield. One flares and streaks across the sky, then another. The streaks thrill her at first, then she remembers that Grandma Coleman said falling stars were one of the Seven Signs of the End of the World and grows uneasy until the next one falls, making her feel small, far away from the sky. She feels every bit of herself pushing against the inside of her skin.

The man in the backseat stops making the sounds. He sits up, claws at the door handle, then a fat hand grips the top of front seat. For a moment he doesn't say anything.

He blinks at Avery.

Where'd you come from? he asks, and even though he tries to say it nicely, the words pile up on the end of his tongue.

Avery doesn't answer. She looks away from the man's face and at the black commas of dirt under the tips of his fingernails. His hand smells of Lava soap.

You must be Madeline's, he says.

She watches him, wishes he'd go back to sleep, wants him to stop talking to her.

You cold?

Avery shakes her head, stares at the ceiling, makes all the tiny holes in it blur together.

The man's arm disappears off the seat, comes back with a green windbreaker. Here, he says. Put this over your legs.

Avery doesn't want the jacket—it smells like cigarettes—but she lets him put it over her.

The man's hand stays on her foot. She pulls her knee up away from it, then the fat fingers brush her ankle, rub her knee. Inside her head she is screaming, *Wake up! Wake up now!*

Shh, he says.

His breath comes down on her, makes her cheeks burn, makes the back of her throat feel like she's swallowed ice. She tries to turn over, away from him, but his other hand comes down on her arm and holds it against the seat.

Shh, he says again, softer this time. His hand moves up, a wedge between her legs.

He whispers, Don't wake up your mama. She'll be mad at us.

Inside her head, the screaming stops. All she hears is the man's breath. She turns her face away from him, looks through the windshield.

The stars are going out. She knows that if she lies there long enough, they all will.

wing

THEY FOLLOW THE river through miles of sage-crusted basalt. Hot wind swirls through the cab, yanks strands of hair from Avery's ponytail, causes Davis to complain that his eyes are burning.

I should have put you in with Lovell, he says over the sound of the wind. The air conditioner works in that one. He points over the steering wheel.

Twenty yards ahead, Lovell drives the hay truck. One corner of the blue tarp that covers the hay has come loose. It snaps in the river of air flowing over the load.

Davis points to the truck again, says, Lovell tied that one down. His voice cuts through the turbulence in the cab. He's getting to where he can't see anymore.

Avery says, I know, but she is thinking that Lovell could probably tie those knots blind. For years, she has watched him tie knots, threading rope or baling twine into bolens and half hitches.

We're going to have to get a couple more loads, Davis says. The price is going to go up in a few weeks unless we get rain.

She nods, says nothing. The hot air makes her sleepy, makes it hard to speak over the noise. She watches the blue wing of tarp ahead.

Davis pulls a stick of gum from his shirt pocket, offers it to Avery. She shakes her head. He pulls off the wrapper and pushes the gum into his mouth.

About time for huckleberries, isn't it? he asks.

Soon, she says. She pictures the buckets of purple berries in the trunk of Mary's car last summer, the day Bernita had gone up the mountain with them—the day Avery first suspected she was pregnant. *Pregnant. Mary. One year,* she thinks.

Davis shifts in the seat, rolls the gum wrapper between a thumb and finger. She knows he is irritated with her. She asks, Did I do something to make you mad?

He shakes his head. No, he says. She watches his shoulders rise, then drop. He flicks the ball of foil out the window.

I just don't know what else to do . . . to help you, he says. I know it's going to take a while to get over this—the baby—but you gotta try to keep living. He glances at her, then looks back at the road.

I don't know, either, she says.

Davis rolls the truck window up, opens the side vent. I can't hear you, he says. He motions toward Avery's window. She finds the crank on the floorboard, fumbles with it. When her window is halfway up, Davis says, Tell me what to do.

I don't know, she says again. If I knew, I'd tell you. Moist heat fills the inside of her shirt.

Maybe we can go somewhere? I can't get away right now. Maybe end of September after things slow down for me?

She smiles at him, shakes her head. It's OK, she says. She watches him worry the side of his face with his hand.

What you're really asking is how long this is going to take—how long it's going to take me to get over this—and I can't tell you that, she says. I wish I knew.

Davis rolls his window down. Noise and hot air again. Avery leans against her own window, closes her eyes, dreams of her father teaching her to tie her shoe. She sits on his lap with her foot resting on his knee. His arms circle her, his hands show her how to loop, wrap, pull.

When she wakes, they are rising out of the river bottom, into open country again. Behind them, Mount Hood, and ahead, foothills rising up into dry, shimmering heat—home.

celilo

L ENNIE DRIVES WEST across the last few miles of
the Plateau before it drops into the wide gorge
cut by the Columbia River.

Salmon will be good for you, she says. Mom says it
will help heal you.

Avery nods. She is dizzy, already tired. This morning, when Lennie had asked her to go to Celilo, she did
not have the energy to come up with a reason to not go.

Lennie says, Davis tells me you haven't been eating
much the past few weeks—ever since you came home.
Your clothes are hanging off you. You have to eat, Avery.

I try, Avery says, and as she says it, she feels pressure
at the back of her throat. Just not hungry.

Well . . . salmon, Lennie says, then, Did you know
that scientists have found the same chemicals that

salmon have in their bodies in the top branches of trees
that grow along the river?

Avery looks at Lennie. She doesn't understand.

When the salmon die and their bodies break down
in the water, part of them goes into the trees—through
the roots.

Oh, Avery says. Oh.

A picture of the tiny white casket in the bottom of
the hole flashes on the back of her brain. She thinks of
the baby there, months from now, thinks of the trees in
the cemetery, thinks of their roots reaching down and
down. She grabs Lennie's arm—hard. She grabs at the
door handle with her other hand.

Lennie brakes, pulls over to the edge of the highway.
The car is still rolling when Avery shoves the door open,
vomits. Yellow bile coats the gravel.

Lennie is out of the car, holding the hair away from
Avery's face. A semi passes, rocking the car, and Avery
retches again. She cannot see, she hears no sound, there
is just the pressure from high in her belly coming again
and again.

When Avery can sit up, Lennie pulls the car forward,
away from the dark spot on the gravel.

Let's get out—get some air.

They stand in brittle grass, just off the edge of the road. Avery feels the heat coming off the pavement, the thrust of hot air from passing traffic.

I'm sorry, Lennie says. I'm so, so sorry. She puts an arm around Avery, draws her close.

Avery shakes her head. I'm alright. I feel better.

AT CELILO, THE water is smooth as a drumhead, except for the place where three ducks drag the skin of the river toward the shore. Downriver, near the bridge, hammers of light strike the water, breaking it into shards.

From the longhouse, the sound of a drum jars the air. The big drum, Lennie calls it. Then the voices, men's and women's, rising, spreading out, moving through the trees in the park.

Lennie and Avery cross the road, walk toward the longhouse. When they enter, Avery feels the sound of the drum, the voices, all the way to the bone.

A circle of women moves around the center pole, around the drum. Some dart like fish in and out of the smoke from cooking fires. Others steer boats on rivers of air, dipping their paddles into the current of sound. Bernita dances with them, smoothing left and right in her wing dress and silver-threaded scarf. The ermine braided into her black hair sway when she moves her head.

The song is over. The women move to the edges of the dirt floor, back to the lawn chairs and benches that surround it, gathering up children, fanning themselves.

Now an elder speaks, her voice steady, strong. She wears a floral scarf on her head, clutches a shawl around her shoulders. *Ce-li-lo* is a ribbon on her tongue, unfolding into the pool of silence that follows, into the space where, once, for her people—Bernita's people—was a second word: *Falls*. The woman's words tell how the men fished from platforms above the sheer drop of roaring water, made their lives around the salmon that came back from the sea.

When she tells about the day the dam was finally complete and the water of the Big River backed up to drown the falls and cover the platforms, her voice trembles. Her hand comes from beneath the shawl, wipes at her face with knobby fingers. The longhouse goes quiet. The air is heavy and thick.

Every year, those salmon came—to pass by—always going back to the same place they were born. Now, there is no place for them to go to.

She wipes her face again. Avery feels a warm tear slide off her own cheek.

THE FIRST BITE of salmon is strong in Avery's mouth. *So many things at once*, she thinks. *Smoke and story*. She takes a second bite. *Water, earth, fire, wind.*

hands

ARLEE'S HOOVES POUND the floor of the horse trailer. Avery feels the trailer shake, feels the rope ripping through her fingers, feels the sheer strength of the horse jerking her arm deeper into the manger. Davis curses, catches the lead rope as Arlee backs out of the trailer. He grips the knot under the horse's chin, yanks him toward the corral.

Forget it, he says.

Across Avery's fingers and palms, a swath of pain. Water gathers into blisters over the raw skin and rims her eyes.

Goddamn, Avery, Davis says as he walks toward her, where are your gloves?

A fist clenches in her stomach. He takes her cupped hand, looks at it, says, You know better.

I didn't have time, she says. I didn't know you were ready to load him and I just didn't think. She feels the ache start up in her right shoulder.

Davis drops her hand, says, Avery, you have to start paying attention or you're going to get hurt. It's time . . . his voice trails off.

I'm going to get some ice, she says, turns away. Tears slide down her face.

I'll just take him over to Lovell's tomorrow, he says. I'll be back later. Behind her, she hears the pickup door slam.

All afternoon, her hands burn. The pain corkscrews through her arms, burrows into her belly. She holds the ice bag with both hands as long as she can stand it, then puts it down, keeps her fingers bent to avoid stretching the damaged skin. She tries to sleep, tries to not think of the way Davis left, waits for the sound of the pickup in the drive. When Lovell calls, she tells him only that Arlee wouldn't load—that Davis will bring him tomorrow.

She stands on the back porch, her hands tucked into her armpits, waiting.

North of town, fields are burning. Gray smoke boils up from the wheat stubble, spreads out, turns the sunlight yellow-brown, gives the air a charred smell.

At feeding time, Avery cannot hold the pitchfork. Arlee and Old Man stand at the fence nickering at her, but she turns away, walks back toward the house.

The sun drops low in the smoke-infused sky, smearing its edges to the color of a ripe peach. A breeze picks up, scuttles dry locust leaves across the gravel driveway, stirs the metallic ribbons she tied to the garden fence last year to scare away birds. Last year—garden.

In the kitchen, she turns on the light over the stove, pulls at the refrigerator door with her fingertips. She finds a spoon in the drainer, eats, lets the cold carton of yogurt cool her hands.

In the living room, she works at twisting the lamp switch. She sits down, holds her palms under the light. The skin over the blisters is translucent, already dying.

Once, Lovell took Avery and Lennie to a rodeo carnival in Grass Valley. After he spent ten minutes tossing Ping-Pong balls at bowls of water with orange petals of fish curled in them, he'd given up, given the girls twenty dollars and walked off toward the beer garden.

Inside the fortune teller's trailer, while she waited for Lennie to have her future told, Avery pictured Grandma Coleman, heard her say *false prophets*, changed her mind even though she had already paid. She didn't want to know her fortune.

Now, she studies the landscape of her hands—the splinters, the ridges of dirt around her nails, and now, the swollen wounds running parallel to her lifelines. She thinks about Lovell's missing finger, Davis's own battered hands, decides that it's not the future that is written on people's hands—that it's the things they love that bruise them, etch history onto their skins.

At 2:45 AM, she lies in the quiet of their room, finally hears the low rumble of the pickup coming around the barn. She waits for the door to slam, but it doesn't, goes to the window, looks out into the yard.

The white sleeve of his shirt flashes in the dark cab. She waits, then moves through the house toward the back door. Cool air swirls through the screen, coils around her bare feet and legs. Layers of smell come in: faint smoke, dry earth, truck exhaust.

The pickup door opens, slams. Davis crosses the dry grass, doesn't see her standing there. She turns.

She stands against the counter, steadies herself, hears him worrying the light switch. The overhead light buzzes. He squints at her, says, You feed? The smell of whiskey hits her.

Couldn't, she says.

He looks at her. Couldn't? he asks. His voice fills the kitchen. She holds out a hand, watches him register what it means.

Christ, too late now, he says. He moves across the floor toward her, falls against her. He moves her hair, breathes into her neck. More whiskey smell.

His hands move over her shoulders and breasts, then under her gown. She feels the places they've touched only after they've moved on, tries to catch up to them but can't. When he lifts her and stumbles toward their bed, she is already lost, left behind in a fortune teller's trailer, waiting, listening to a rattling air conditioner.

may 1978

THE AFTERNOON so clear Avery can see a hundred miles across the Plateau, all the way to Mount Hood. On the other side of the pickup seat, Davis, just old enough to have his driver's license, steers with his right hand, his left arm out the window, index finger hooked around the mirror brace. *Old rancher already*, Avery thinks.

They are still giddy with distance and summer, giddy that Paul has lent them the truck, trusted them to make the trip by themselves. On the way to drop Lennie at the airport, Avery sat in the middle of the seat. Now, with Lennie gone and her scooted back to the passenger side, she misses the heat of Davis's thigh against hers.

Last week, she and Lennie were on their way to Fletcher when they passed Davis on River Road. He honked the truck horn, lifted his hand off the wheel, waved.

That boy likes you, Lennie said as they leaned into a curve.

Avery felt something start in her chest, a small bird waking, and wondered whether it was because of Lennie's driving or what Lennie had just said.

Of course he does. Most of the time, she said. We grew up together.

That's not what I meant and you know it. Lennie jabbed Avery's arm with her finger.

I don't think so, Avery said.

Lennie licked her fingers, smoothed the edge of a feather hanging from the rearview, said, Uh huh. You ought to see how he looks at you now! Anybody looking would notice.

I don't know, Avery said, and the saying of it meant two things: She didn't know if he liked her for sure, and she didn't know what to do if what Lennie said was true.

I don't think it works that way, she said. People don't know each other for five years and suddenly decide they love each other. Not in *that* way, anyway.

Do you really believe that?

Yeah, Avery said. It's the other way around. People stop loving each other after enough time goes by.

Hell! Lennie said. I know that Mom and Dad
still love each other, even though they won't admit it.
It's just too hard for them to live together—both too
stubborn.

Avery thought of her own parents—Madeline,
Frank. Her eyes stung. She looked through the cracked
windshield at Paul and Mary's porch, at Paul's white
stump socks strung across the back clothesline like bril-
liant teeth.

They were almost to the driveway before Lennie
spoke again. Ask him, then, she said. You watch and see
if I'm not right. He likes you.

Avery knew she wouldn't ask. She watched the row
of teeth coming closer. If he does like me, he'll have to
tell me, she said.

Now, WITH LENNIE gone off to Salt Lake to a powwow,
silence stretches between Avery and Davis, fills the truck
cab. She takes a novel out of her bag, opens it, tries to
read. She feels him looking at her.

Summer reading list for freshman English. *The Old
Man and the Sea*, she says. You read it?

No. We had to read *The Great Gatsby* in sopho-
more English. Davis nods his head sideways toward the
book. He lived in Idaho, he says, adds, Killed himself.

I know.

She studies the side of his face, the fine light hair on his jawline, and just now, a faint patch of heat surfacing from under the skin of his cheek.

Besides the sea, what's it about? he asks.

Not sure yet. I'm only a few pages in, but I like it so far. It's easy to read.

Read me some?

Avery has never read to anyone besides teachers, Grandma Coleman, Mary. She opens the book, begins. He reaches across the space between them, lays his hand on her arm.

Wait, he says. Something just behind her navel stretches its wings, turns, lifts. She closes the book, pulls it against her, covers the spot where the bird has risen higher, into her rib cage.

Davis finds a turnout, parks Paul's pickup just off the shoulder. He leans against the door, tries to find a place to rest his hands, finally hangs them from the bottom of the steering wheel.

OK. Now, he says, nodding toward Avery and the book again.

She is self-conscious, wishes he hasn't asked her to read, but she begins again. She reads about the old man and the boy and their bad luck. Reading about the man's scarred-up hands, she thinks of Lovell's hands.

She feels Davis looking at her again, looks up from the page. He smiles. Heat fills his cheeks again. Wings stretch inside her.

Avery reads on, knowing that later, she will have to go back and read the pages again, because she has stopped paying attention to the story, now that she's just filling the pickup cab with her voice.

When she looks at him again, she thinks he might be asleep. His head rests against the doorframe, eyes are closed, but his thumbs rub back and forth on the steering wheel. When he realizes she's stopped reading, he opens his eyes. It occurs to her that, at some time, she has turned her body completely toward him. Their knees almost touch—a synapse waiting.

Does this old man have a name? he asks.

I peeked ahead, and I don't think so.

I like it better that way, he says.

You want me to keep reading?

Yep. Before we lose our light.

Through the rearwindow, Avery sees the sun is much lower than when they'd parked. She can still see the top of Mount Hood, rising out of a cloud bank like

an island in a sea of sky. She begins to read again, set-
tling into the rhythm of the words, letting the language
even out her breath, falling in love with the sound of the
word *sargasso*.

bodies in motion

THIN DAGGERS OF ice fall through the air, poke Avery's face. She tightens the knot on her scarf, tucks the ends down inside her coat collar, struggles to keep her balance while Davis steers the truck over rocks and frozen dirt, too sick to do anything but drive.

The orange baling twine pops as she cuts it. She jams the knife blade into an unopened bale, leaving it there until she needs it again, grabs the ends of the twine and pulls it free.

The roping gloves she grabbed on the way out of the house are stiff and wet. She pushes flakes of hay off the flatbed with her hands, shoves it with her boots, releasing the brief scent of summer into the bitter wind. Bawling cows lumber in to eat, picking up a stitch in the seam of Black Angus that stretches out behind the truck. When the bales are fed out, she huddles against the cab.

Small bits of straw and pea hay swirl up off the flatbed, stick to her wet face and coat.

Davis yells Hold on! through the open truck window. Avery stands up, her feet wide. She pounds twice on the pickup's roof, holds onto the metal rack welded to its cab. When he turns the truck and starts down the slope, she is disoriented by the suddenness of tree line and sky.

THE COTTON THREADS of her gloves leave a grid pattern on the icy pickup door handle. Inside the cab, she swipes at the windshield with a rag she finds on the seat. Davis rolls up his window. Now she can smell the beer.

At the shed, they load the truck again. Sweat gathers at Davis's temples. His skin is pale against the brown canvas of his coat.

They top the hill above the Farrow lease, the river bottom pasture where Davis keeps the bulls. Dark shapes amble through the next field—on the wrong side of the fence—heads bent, grazing on green blades of winter wheat.

Davis hits the steering wheel with the flat of his hand. Goddamnit! he yells.

The air shatters. Shards of Davis's words cut through her clothes, gash the skin of her chest. Cold air rushes through the wounds.

On the day her father came home from the field
and found Madeline sitting by the couch where she had
laid Jean Ann, he called the sheriff and waited on the
front porch. After the ambulance took Jean Ann away,
after Dr. Platt had sent her mother drifting on a tide of
tranquilizers, Avery sat on the porch, shivering from the
needles of sun piercing her skin, waiting for someone to
ask her what happened.

Then, she heard her father's voice in the kitchen. It
was his telephone voice, but he laid out his words slow
and quiet like he did when he talked to horses. She heard
her own name and the word *tomorrow*.

When Frank came outside and walked past her,
his fingertips brushed across the top of her head like a
breeze. At the bottom of the steps, he turned, pointed at
the kitchen door.

Go in there and find something to eat, he said.
Grandma'll be here tomorrow.

When she thought of food, something sour pushed
up from her stomach, pressed her throat. She stayed put,
stared down into the empty cup of a purple iris.

Avery worked at sliding time back into place, shifting fragments around like the plastic tiles in the frame
puzzle Grandma Coleman kept on her coffee table. She
couldn't make it come out right. Sometimes, she could

get the parts of the day to meet at one edge, but then everything else would be out of place. Oatmeal, warm porch boards, red throbbing light in the yard—washing machine. Now, now, three couch cushions propped in the swing, dripping, dripping water through the wooden slats. Then, from the direction of the running ditch, the sound of rocks smashing into water and her father's voice yelling Goddamn! Goddamn!

DAVIS TURNS THE pickup around, says, I'm going home to get Old Man—get those bulls back in.

He takes the road that runs along the railroad tracks. Fist-sized chunks of gravel make a boiling sound under the tires. Davis runs his hand across the shadow of hair on his chin, does not speak.

They follow the river bottom west, passing leafless underbrush and islands of snow with their stands of red willow streaming blood-colored light. Avery closes her eyes, lulled by the whir of the truck heater.

She feels the train before she hears it—a bullet moving toward them from a hundred yards down the track. Davis sits forward in the seat, pushes the gas pedal. She tries to figure the distance between them and the crossing.

The train shoots toward them, the white-hot lamp on its engine a comet. Avery does not speak—knows it won't do any good. She grabs the door handle. Fifty yards.

The train whistle sounds. She feels Davis's body contract, become a solid object hurtling toward the screaming train. At fifteen yards, he brakes. The loaded pickup skids past the crossing, fishtails, stops. In the next instant, they are submerged in a wall of vibration and sound. Avery pictures them going up in a spray of flesh and metal.

Neither of them speaks. Avery's cheeks ignite. Heat spreads through her limbs.

Davis opens the truck door, steps out, bends over. She watches him retch.

Her heart pulses against her breastbone, inside the skin of her wrists. Her arms are weightless—she feels as if they might detach, float away. She hears the throb of blood against her eardrums.

Goddamn, she says into the ringing air. Goddamn.

august 1970

COB WAVES HIS arms, clutches a thick black Bible with scrubbed hands that still show crescents of coal dust under the nails. He stands in the middle of Aunt Velvie's living room, sweat streaming down his temples, combed-back hair shining under the overhead bulb, preaching to the family, neighbors that fill the rooms of the house, spill out onto porches.

His voice scares Avery. It is like the thunder that rolled out of the head of the hollow yesterday bringing first the scent, then the smell of rain, then him home from the mine, covered in black dust, his pink lips, green eyes shining out through white rings of skin around them. Aunt Laurel drew him a bath, moved pots of steaming water from the stove to the washtub on the kitchen floor, added cold water dipped from the well bucket. Through the closed door, swish and pour of water, laughter, low talking, silence, then Laurel opening the door, carrying a pile of dirty clothes out to the back porch, smiling.

christmas tree

FROM THE KITCHEN, the creak of a thermos handle, then the hard closing of the back door. Cold
air surges into the living room, eddies around
Avery, worries the tinsel on the Christmas tree. She hears
the pickup engine catch and slide into gear, hears Davis
drive away, gone off to feed cattle and rehang a gate
in the Eighty. Then, except for wood sputtering in the
stove, the place goes still.

He did not ask her to go with him today—has not
asked for days—and she did not offer to go.

Avery lies down on the couch, pulls fistfuls of quilt
up under her chin. She does not feel like working or call-
ing Lennie. She wants to sleep.

The quilt smells like Davis—like dust and sweat, his sleep. She feels the weight of it settle over her, lets it anchor her in the silence.

When she wakes, the room is cool. She pushes a chunk of tamarack into the stove, goes to the kitchen for tea. The floor by the kitchen sink is wet. Coffee. She says, Damnit, Davis, yanks off her socks, lays them on the hearth to dry.

She pulls gift boxes from under the tree. In one, she finds the pair of elkskin gloves she gave Davis for Christmas. She folds the tree skirt, made from an old tablecloth, sets it on the couch.

When she opens the spare room door, cold air and the odor of fresh paint rush out. Avery tugs the window curtain to let in light, swipes dead flies off the sill, turns. Her eyes adjust. Crib, willow rocker, stick horse in the corner. A yellow crocheted blanket with a brittle moth stuck to it.

She gathers decoration boxes from the closet. Before she leaves the room, she stops to press her hand into the crib mattress. All the way back to the living room, she hears—still feels—the sound of the plastic cracking her palm.

Avery lifts ornaments off the dried-out tree limbs. She wraps Caroline's feathered birds in tissue, lays them in an old Christmas card box. She places jewel-colored balls in their worn cartons—fading planets glow from paper towel nests. She stacks Mary's tatted snowflakes in a bracelet box, rubber bands the torn lid, drops fistfuls of tinsel into a pile on the floor. She unwinds the strings of lights, thinks of the Christmas tumbleweed hanging from Lovell's ceiling, every year the same, nothing else on it but clear, white light.

Avery takes pieces of the carved Nativity scene off the bookshelf, counts a year for each piece she places in the box, begins with the green-robed Wise Man Lovell added this year, remembers what he said when he handed it to her: I'll just keep adding until I can't whittle anymore. No telling what kind of animals will show up.

She counts back to the baby in the manger he gave her that first Christmas at Paul and Mary's house—this house.

The tree makes a trail of needles across the rug, across the kitchen floor. Outside, she hacks at the limbs with Davis's machete, then gathers them, throws them on the burn pile to rust until spring. She hacksaws the trunk into foot-long sections until the dampness of her shirt, the coldness of her feet, bare inside the rubber boots, registers. She hangs the saw on a locust branch, walks back to the house. Behind her, a spray of needles, the scattered vertebrae of the tree on the snow.

dishpan

ANXIETY KNOTS HER stomach, tangles her nerves like the tattered blackberry bushes in the ditch. She makes the turn, follows the frost-ridged gravel around the barn. No lights in the house, no porch light, but Davis's pickup in the driveway. Avery feels the knot loosen.

Her headlights slice across the yard, graze a metal object on the porch steps, light up the side of the truck. She sees the icy mud and dry grass plastered to its bumper, the scraped and dented driver's side door. Anger spreads through her.

Arlee and Old Man nicker, pace the fence line. Their hooves thud against the frozen ground. Avery drives back to the barn, aims the headlights toward the feeder. She forks in a large flake of hay with trembling, bare hands. She listens to the horses chew, watches hay chaff swirl in the headlights, tries to even out her breath.

At the edge of the porch, Grandma Coleman's dishpan sits on the uneven boards. Avery climbs the steps, looks down into the pan. In the darkness, she can only make out a faint sheen of liquid. She nudges it with her foot. Water sloshes out onto her boot tip.

She'd taken the round aluminum pan from Grandma's place when she and Madeline cleaned up after the funeral. At the time, Madeline had said, Of all things. Now, what would you want with that old pan?

Avery didn't feel like explaining how the sound of it banging against a counter or the bottom of a sink was a comfort—how the soft thud of dishes against the inside, the heat of the water it held, the warm metal smell were markers, things she could count on. Instead, she'd joked that maybe she'd want it for a foot washing at church.

Inside the back door, a cocoon of familiar smells: damp wool and smoke-infused canvas, then the kitchen: coffee and bacon grease, sharper in the cold air of a house that has gone unheated for a while.

A dim lightbulb burns over the stove. She calls out his name, moves through the kitchen. In the living room, she feels him, then hears the sound of his sleep, deep whiskey sleep: long pulls of air into his chest, breath pausing then rushing back out in short puffs. She moves toward the couch, where he usually sleeps, puts out her hand, but he is not there.

Avery hears the back door open, the snap of the light switch, Lovell's voice, Jesus.

In the light that washes through the doorway, she sees Davis in the recliner, shirtless, his head bent forward and to the right. His boots and pants are muddy, his right arm slung over the side of the chair, bloody between the wrist and elbow. He's had to pull a calf.

From the kitchen, Lovell again, Je-sus God, then, Avery?

She is close enough now to smell the manure on Davis's boots, the stale aluminum breath. She touches him, holds her hand to the cool skin of his chest. His breath shifts beneath her fingers.

She wipes spit off his shoulder with the hem of her shirt, turns toward Lovell's voice. The fluorescent light has not yet come full on, but she can make out the bloody dish towel under the table, the smears of blood on the linoleum and countertops—Davis's blood.

He in there? Lovell lifts his hand toward the living room.

Avery nods.

Passenger window's busted on the pickup. Dead calf in the bed.

Lovell switches on the table lamp by the recliner. Avery checks Davis's arm. The streaks are dark and dry. Blood and manure.

Lovell lifts the other arm, says, Can you get me more light? Avery pulls the ceiling fan chain. Weak light and cold air fall over the room. Another towel lies on the floor by the recliner, a soaked-red petal on the faded rug.

Lovell holds Davis's arm straight out. Rivulets of blood have thickened around the wound.

He's going to need stitches. Lovell pushes the skin around the finger-long gash, moves his face closer to it. Glass, he says. Do you have any peroxide? He nods toward the cut. If you do, put some on this arm. I'm going to go start the truck.

Avery pulls the afghan over Davis's chest. From the kitchen, Lovell yells, Call Lennie and tell her to come over here and build a fire while we're gone!

The wound fizzes when she pours the peroxide over it. Davis stirs, shifts his feet, goes back to sleep.

Avery flips on the bedroom light. Rumpled quilt on the bed. A wadded pair of muddy white socks on the floor. He has slept in here, she says aloud.

She rummages, finds a work shirt with snaps. Lovell helps her dress Davis, rolls the cuff of the shirt above the wound. Together, they walk him down the back steps. In the porch light, a skin of ice on the water in the dishpan.

WHEN THEY COME home just before daylight, the water in the pan has frozen solid. Ice pushes at its sides and bottom, changes its shape forever. Inside the blood-tinged ice, a blue cloud of fabric—the Pendleton shirt Avery gave him for Christmas.

the orchard

AVERY FINDS MADELINE in the orchard—a puppet propped against a snow-blasted tree trunk—legs stretched out in front of her, scraped and bloody hands resting on the ground. Sprigs of hair jut from her braid like lightning.

Avery kneels by Madeline, glances around, does not find a liquor bottle, sees the small heap of apples beside her, winter-bloated, the color of rust.

Mom, Avery says. Madeline does not answer.

Avery cups her mother's shivering hand, looks for the wound. The fingers are smeared with rotten apple. Dirt shows under the nails, flecks the shallow trenches of the scrapes.

Madeline breathes through her mouth. Stale air—
she hasn't been drinking. Avery feels fear launch out of
her chest, into her limbs.

Can you stand up? Avery asks. She shows her mother
Davis's wool coat, grabbed off its peg on her way out of
the house.

Madeline grunts when Avery touches her arm, but
she stands, lets Avery help her into the coat.

Mom, are you sick? Where's your coat?

Madeline looks at Avery with dull eyes. Apples, she
says, then, No sack.

Let's get to the house, Avery says.

Apples, Madeline says. Under the snow. She leans
against Avery, lets her lead her through the orchard, out
of reach of the bony-fingered trees.

MADELINE STANDS AT the sink, lets Avery pour peroxide
over her hands, watches the blood wash away.

It's not too bad, Avery says.

Madeline stares at her frothing palms, says, Yeah, I
said unto thee when thou wast in thy blood, live.

What? Avery asks.

Upon Christ's grave, three roses bloom, she says.

Crystals of fear form in Avery's fingers. They tremble as she dabs the wounds with a paper towel. She leads Madeline to a chair, sits down at the table, too.

Madeline looks at her palms again, then at Avery, says, My grand-mommy was a blood stopper. Could stop blood, just like that. She closes a hand, snaps a finger. Her eyes are brighter, her voice more musical. There is movement in her hands now, color in her face. Avery hopes she is back from wherever she was before. She listens to her mother, tries to steer her own mind away from a tangle of questions.

People would call on her, and she'd go. No matter where or what time. She could stop it by walking east and saying Ezekiel 16:6. I saw her do it. Woman from Holden sent her boy, said she'd had a nosebleed for three days. Grand-mommy went over there and stopped it. She knew the roots, too. She could cure about anything . . .

Avery hears Davis's pickup come around the barn. When he comes into the kitchen, he looks at Avery and Madeline, the paper towels on the sink, the peroxide. He raises his eyebrows.

She fell down, Avery says.

Madeline looks at Davis, says, I had me two girls once. Least one died—drowned in the Buffalo Creek flood.

Avery feels lightheaded, feels the question take hold, feels the taproot spear into her brain.

january 1972

AVERY STANDS ON the bed, traces a finger through water droplets on the window. Cold air licks at her ankles. She lifts a pillow with her toes, shoves both feet under it.

On the other side of the glass, watery darkness in the backyard, the outline of Paul's pickup, chicken coop, a brittle rim of wheat stubble. Then, a heavier darkness presses down on the field, the trees—anchoring them in blackness. Avery pictures her house beyond the irrigation ditch, imagines the point where light would burn through Madeline's bedroom window if she were home.

From the doorway, Mary's voice. What are you doing? Get under those covers before you get chilled. Then plump hands pull the quilt over Avery, leaving the faint scent of dish soap.

Stay under those covers. It'll soon warm up in here, Mary says, then turns back toward the door.

Avery hears her sit down in her recliner, hears her murmuring to Paul.

THE SOUND OF the telephone reaches into Avery's sleep—she sits up.

In the dresser mirror, an orange smear of light. Voices. Truck door.

She stands, swipes at the window with the sleeve of her gown. Fire. Other side of the trees. A house. It's across the ditch. Her house.

Red taillights of Paul's pickup bounce down the frozen driveway. More flashes of red out on the main road. Fire engines.

Avery's legs go icy as she turns to jump off the bed. Mary scoops her up, sets her on the floor, leads her into the bright light of the kitchen. She pulls Avery onto her lap, says, You know your mama isn't home. Don't cry, sweetheart. She's safe. She'll be fine.

Mary rocks her, smoothing her hair, folding her into the flannel bathrobe she wears. Avery can't stop the tears burning down her cheeks, soaking the collar of her gown.

Mary pulls a tissue out of the robe pocket, wipes a string of snot from Avery's nose, says, You're going to cry yourself sick. A dull pain pounds in Avery's forehead.

The phone rings. I have to get that, Mary says. She sets Avery on the cold floor. Go lay down on the couch. Cover up. I'll be there directly.

Avery wobbles through the living room, toward her bedroom window. She climbs back onto the bed, puts her face close to the cold glass, watches spears of flame cut through the house, reach out, up, light the sky. She tries to get her breath to catch, even out.

In the kitchen, Mary says, Thank the Lord, into the telephone, then she is behind Avery, leading her away from the window again.

AVERY WAKES, NOT knowing where she is. Weak daylight around the edges of the drapes. Coughing in the bathroom—Paul. She registers the wet, smoky smell hanging in the air, remembers.

Mary is at the cookstove, stirring gravy. She turns, smiles, says, Good morning. No school today. She points toward the window, says, Snow, then points again, toward Paul's smoke-smudged coat hanging over a chair. That thing stinks, doesn't it? Take it out back, will you?

The coat is soaked, heavy. Avery holds it to her chest, starts for the back room. By the door, a cardboard box. In it, toys, books, Avery's clothes from home—all clean, dry. Things she thought burned up in the night.

Avery picks up Jean Ann's talking doll, carries it to the kitchen, stands behind Mary with it hanging from her hand.

Mary lays the wooden spoon across the rim of the skillet, turns, says, Paul found it. That box was sitting out on the porch this morning.

tumbleweeds

THE TUMBLEWEEDS BURN hot. Avery drops them into the flames, watches them blossom into dahlias of fire until she has to turn away from the heat.

The line of brown and black weeds stretches along the north and east sides of the waterlogged corral at the edge of cow camp. All winter, wind pushed them across the flats until they were trapped, piled deep in the corner, a froth of brittle branches.

Now, Avery tries to keep her promise to have the corral clean and ready for horses when Davis and Lovell get back from gathering cows and calves. She pulls at the dried stems, hears the snap and give of tangled skeletons as she mashes them between the palms of her gloves. The branches scratch at her face and wrists, tangle in her boot strings as she tries to walk. By the time she gets back to the fire, all that is left of the last ones are gray flecks riding the updrafts.

She checks her watch. In two hours, the sun will fall out of the gray sky, taking the light with it. She calculates how long the men have been gone, decides they should be back by now.

Inside the camp trailer, the smell of mildew, the vinegar of Davis's dirty socks. She hears the wind pick up, notices Davis's slicker wadded up on the seat cushion. She grabs it and heads out into the damp wind.

Lovell's pickup starts on the first try. She crosses the highway, tries to see through the smear of water left by a ragged windshield wiper.

Two gates. The wood posts are slick in her hands, the second one hard to close. She yanks on the post, stretching out the slack, strains until she is able to drop the hook over the top.

She drives across the field, dodging rocks and sagebrush, scanning the skyline. Davis and Lovell are out there, somewhere between the highway and the bluffs that drop forty feet into the Columbia. She knows they are wet and cold, hopes to find them before the dark settles down into the bare, nest-clotted trees.

Cattle clump beneath cottonwoods and locusts. Avery slows, checks for ear tags on the calves, drives on.

She pushes the heater lever all the way over, turns the radio knob. The station out of Pasco calls for rain and low temperatures. No kidding, she says.

She finds them near the bluff, stops a distance away to watch. Ruby darts between their horses and the cow they're trying to separate from her calf—a Hereford Avery recognizes, knows by several names: Number 329, Fence Jumper, and Lovell's own favorite, Hellbitch.

The confused calf, not long on the ground, weaves back and forth between its mother and the horses.

Davis's first loop misses. He gathers the rope, trots Old Man in a wide circle, closes in. Lovell holds Arlee between the cow and calf. Davis throws again. When the calf is down, Lovell hands him a syringe, turns his head and torso to watch for the cow. In that moment—that movement, Avery sees Lovell as an old man for the first time.

When the cow charges, Lovell and Arlee whirl around to face her. She stops, ignores Ruby who arcs around her, trying to turn her away from the men. She twists her head from side to side, pushes a sound from deep in her belly. A ribbon of slobber flies from her mouth.

Avery watches Davis speak to her while he works the calf, knows he's probably saying, Alright mama, like always. He puts in the ear tag, lets the calf up. It trots over to its mother, nuzzles her teat.

When the men notice her, Avery waves, holds up the thermos. She watches Davis pull the rope back into a coil and hang it on the saddle, waits to see whether he will ride over, knows that either way, it will break her heart.

signs and wonders

AVERY COMES ACROSS the book under a scatter of magazines on the waiting room table, recognizes the weight of it, the yellow-lettered title on its front: *The Bible Story*. She brushes her fingers over its sky-blue cover. It is slick and perfect in her hands—familiar.

She holds the book out to Madeline. Look, she says, Do you remember when Grandma bought these for us?

Madeline frowns, says, Us? She stares at Avery with dull eyes, fiddles with the latch on her purse.

Me—and Jean Ann. They came in the mail.

Long time, Madeline says. She opens and closes the latch, hums.

Avery opens the book, tries to shut out the sounds of the waiting room, the sound of her sister's name—Madeline's red suitcase on the floor. A familiar scent rises from the pages, the pure Sunday school smell of everything right and good and terrible in the world. She recognizes story titles and scenes, pictures of people in jewel-colored robes, their expectant faces washed in concentrated light—others scenes of anguished people, roiling darkness.

She finds the picture of Adam in the Garden, registers a flicker of childish shame, realizes he isn't as naked as he seemed those years ago—notices that the lion's head conceals his lower body. She smiles, remembers overhearing Grandma Coleman once blurt out to Mary that she'd never seen Grandpa without clothes—that he'd always undressed in the dark—remembers the embarrassment she felt at thinking of Grandma and Grandpa like that.

Madeline shifts in her seat, points to the clock. They're late, she says.

Maybe they're just running behind, Avery says. She lays the book on the magazines, opens the folder from Dr. Blackerby's office. Madeline's file is now filled with lab reports, forms, doctors' notes containing phrases that echo Dr. Blackerby's words: *malnutrition, loss of intellectual functioning, alcoholic dementia.* Avery closes the file, closes her eyes.

Madeline leans across Avery, picks up the *Bible Story* book. She opens it, chops it softly with her hand, says, There will be signs on the sun, the moon, and in the stars.

Avery recognizes the language of Grandma Coleman's End of the World speeches, Uncle Cob's front room sermons.

A woman in a denim jumper opens a door, calls Madeline's name. Avery stands, picks up her mother's suitcase. Madeline holds the open book against her chest. She looks at the woman, then at Avery.

OK, Mom, Avery says. Let's go. They follow the woman down a hall toward the intake office—Madeline clutching the book, Avery, the file.

There will be wars and rumors of wars, Madeline says.

meridian

THEY CROSS THE 45th parallel, drive east toward a line of clouds that drag gray tentacles across dry land. Avery cannot smell the rain yet—how it sifts through sagebrush and jackpine, reaches into the sand and dirt of the far hills, gathers a stone-hard scent, lifts it into the wind.

Rain, Madeline says.

Mmmm. About time.

We used to run from it, Madeline says. Could smell it coming—a different kind of smell than here—and we'd run up the holler to the house and put on our swimsuits, then we'd run down the holler—meet it. Lord God, it was cold—felt like ice hitting our skin, and if you had a sunburn, worse.

She stops talking, looks out the window.

Past Baker City, the rain stops. Hills, long curves, then the land opens up north and east, stretches ahead into Idaho. The flat places remind Avery of home, of fields that say, Something happened here—places where a moment ago there was noise and commotion, now, empty, still.

THE ROOM IS small. Just inside the door, a twin bed. On it, a still, human curve beneath a Day-Glo afghan. Beside it, an orange vinyl chair full of stuffed animals.

Across the room, another bed—Madeline's—made up military style, a bare wall marked by pale outlines, the ghosts of picture frames.

Madeline stands by the empty bed, arms limp. A young woman in purple scrubs pulls the wrapper off a plastic tub, sets it on the bed. This is your welcome package, she says. She picks a round yellow sticker off the wrapper, sticks it on a chart labeled *Shorter*, clipped to the bathroom door.

Madeline looks into the tub, picks up a comb, then a yellow denture box. She opens and closes it.

Let me help you get settled, the assistant says. Did you bring any furniture from home?

No, Avery says. She opens Madeline's red suitcase, lays the underwear, T-shirts, jeans in metal drawers, hangs two blouses in the closet, makes a note to find something to bring from home—a photo or knickknack, a plant—something to warm Madeline's side of the room.

Madeline sits down on the bed. Avery kneels, takes off her mother's tennis shoes, puts them on the closet floor. She helps Madeline put on the hospital slippers from the tub, stands up.

I'm going to go finish up the paperwork, she says.

The assistant smiles at Avery, then Madeline, says, She'll be fine.

When Avery comes back to the room, the woman in the first bed has not moved. Madeline is in bed, too, her back to the door—another curve. The nurse's aid writes on a chart. Her vitals look good, she says.

Avery goes to Madeline, leans over her, says, I'll be back in the morning, Mom. Madeline does not speak. She turns her head toward Avery, lifts her hand from under the blanket, holds out the yellow denture box.

the red slip

I N THE RAGS to Riches thrift store, she scoots hangers across the rod, finds the slip—a secret wedged between dresses and blouses.

In the fitting room, the blood-red rayon burns in her hands. She gathers it into a wreath, drops it over her head. It falls, forms to the curves of her waist and hips. Fire and ice, a shock of satin that stops just above her knees.

She turns, looks into the narrow mirror on the door, lays her hands on her concave belly, feels them rise and fall as she breathes.

She is a lit fuse.

july 1983

MARY IS PROPPED upright in the bed, eyes closed, someplace else. Davis sits hump-shouldered in a plastic chair by the window, hands tucked between his knees, dusty boots splayed out in front of him. When he sees Avery come in, he lifts his eyebrows, smiles.

Hot out there, she says.

The sound of the room has changed in the hour she was away, the sound of machines replaced by Mary's ragged breath.

Avery bends down, kisses Davis's oily forehead.

I hate this place, he says.

I know, she says, wonders if Mary can hear them.

They came and took the monitor off, breathing tube. The doctor says it will be tonight or tomorrow morning.

Avery feels all the air go out of her, tries to hold the sound inside, still thinks Mary might hear. She clamps her jaw, headache already beginning.

Why the iv? she whispers.

They left it to give her medicine to keep her comfortable, he says, rubs his right thumb back and forth over the palm of his left hand.

In the hall, the sound of dinner carts rolling past Mary's door.

You need to eat, Avery says.

He shakes his head, points across the room toward a table, There's coffee and tea over there.

On a table across the room, a tray with a coffee pot, tea bags, a carafe of hot water. Avery makes a cup of tea because she's chilled from the air conditioner—because she doesn't know what else to do.

SHEET LIGHTNING BEHIND her eyes. A flash—yesterday afternoon, seeing Mary through the kitchen window, standing in the garden, her arms limp, swollen feet and ankles rising over the tops of her tennis shoes. The green sweater she wore hung from her now-small frame, sagged at the hem. Paul's sweater. When Avery went to her, she found Mary collapsed, folded into herself, like she'd meant to lie down, sleep among the stalks and trickling vines.

Ten months before, it was Mary who found Paul on the back porch settee one morning, head thrown back, eyes open, his newspaper drifting across the yard, catching on the fence. She'd buried him out on Paradise Bench, frost burning the edges of the flowers they piled over him.

Mary's moves her head, moans. Davis stands, leans over her, rubs the parchment on the back of her hand. It's OK, Grammie, we're here. It's OK.

Avery studies her washed-out face, the thread of scar at the corner of her right eye, broken capillaries on her cheeks. The black stubble on Mary's chin makes her look away.

Caroline pushes open the door, comes inside carrying a vase of daisies. She says, Oh. Avery feels lightning strike just behind her left eye.

MORE PEOPLE IN the room, more voices that stop when the night nurse opens the door. She takes Mary's pulse, lifts the blanket, wraps her hand around a puffy ankle. She tucks the blanket around Mary's leg, asks, Does anyone need anything? On the way out of the room, she lifts the coffee pot, shakes it, carries it out with her.

When the nurse is gone, Avery touches Mary's foot, can feel its coldness through the blanket. She wraps her hand around Mary's. Cold.

Caroline is telling a story about a whipping Mary gave her when she was little—something about shoe polish. Everyone else is laughing when Avery feels Mary go. No moan, no death rattle, just a small absence Avery can feel through her fingers. She has to say it twice before anyone hears her.

artifacts

THIS MORNING, THE near bed is empty, the covers pulled up, afghan folded on the chair. Madeline sits on the edge of her own bed, feet resting on a plastic stool, fingers worrying the hem of the white sheet. Her hair is loose, damp. Steel-colored strands hang down her back, wet her gown.

Until Madeline got sick, Avery had scarcely seen her mother without braids, usually only on mornings after she stayed out all night, came home with her hair loose and wild. Or the day after Jean Ann died, when Madeline woke and started to howl again—when Frank gave her another one of the pills Dr. Blackerby had left. After that, she slept all day, drifted away again, her hair flared on the pillow like one of Grandma Coleman's black dahlias.

Mom, did you sleep OK? Avery asks.

Noisy, Madeline says. Lights. *Squeak, squeak, squeak* all night long.

Avery takes a brush from her purse, works it through the ends of Madeline's hair. Did you like your breakfast? she asks.

Madeline's voice is brighter now. How's that man of yourn?

Avery drops the rhythm of the brush strokes, picks it up again. Fine, she says. Building fence.

Tell him he needs to come check my outside spigots, she says. I heared 'em humming in the night.

Avery nods, pictures the museum inside her mother's head, where she must spend her days rifling though boxes in basement storerooms, pulling out pictures and jagged shards of artifacts, holding them up to the light.

I don't like it here, Madeline says. They don't feed me.

Sure they feed you, Avery says. The aide told me you ate most of your breakfast.

Hair is a woman's crowning glory, her mother says.

Avery puts the brush in her purse, sits in the orange chair. A tear slides down Madeline's cheek. She says, Your daddy'll come home. He's just put out with me for what happened to the house.

Avery feels something—a small bird—stir in her rib cage.

Madeline twists the sheet in her hands, says, I found his wedding ring—in a coffee can in the shed. I went to look for a nail . . . Her voice drops away, her mouth keeps working. She releases the sheet, traces a vein on the back of her hand.

I knew for sure he'd left me then. Another tear, and another, then she is silent.

Mama, do you need anything? Avery asks. She hands Madeline a tissue.

Uh uh, she says.

Avery watches her mother pull the tissue apart, push the shreds around on her lap. When she lifts her face, the landscape is changed—clouds passing over. She is gone again.

You got any babies, yet?

Avery feels the pulse in her eardrums—like being underwater.

No, she says.

Oh, Madeline says, then, I'm tired. She lies back on the bed. Avery pulls the covers over her, asks, Are you warm enough? Do you want me to close the curtains?

Tell your daddy to get home. I can't find Jean Ann. I've looked and looked . . .

The end of her sentence thins out, slices into Avery's chest. I will, she says, then, I'll be back soon, Mama.

OK, Madeline says. Hurry, honey.

Avery is reaching for the door handle when she hears her mother say, It weren't your fault, you know. Weren't your fault.

spring 1968

S HE HOOKS HER fingers in her father's belt loops, holds on, tries to not slide off the tops of his boots. One, two, three—one, two, three. He rocks from foot to foot, gestures with the bottle of beer he holds, sings along with the record player. She can smell the diesel oil in the dark fabric of his pants.

Draping across Madeline's lap, Jean Ann, wearing a nightgown, twisting her hair.

Frank drags out the last notes. The bee-oo-ti-full Tenn-ess-eeeeee Wallllll-tz! He throws back his head, laughs.

Madeline shakes her head, closes her eyes.

on greasewood creek

ON GREASEWOOD CREEK, Davis and Lovell are horseback in the uphill corner of the pasture, waiting for the bulls to calm enough to drive them down the fence line and into the Eighty, where cows shade up in dark islands of sumac. Wind twists through the Russian olives, gathering a scent like the sea, coming to Avery, causing her to conjure a ship, just sailed away, rising on the swell of open ground between her and the men, passing them and disappearing over the ridgeline. In the tall grasses, remnants of the launching—scraps of white morning glory, tangled ribbons of purple vetch, yellow Mexican hat flowers caught on the heads of rye and timothy.

The creek still runs, late for this time of year. When the wind lulls, she can hear it. She turns her head away from the pickup and horse trailer and from the men, ignores the feathered jet trails in the sky. She feels time rise up and follow the ship. Memory goes, too, leaving a recognition that does not need naming. Avery is present and feeling, swelling into the hollow places of her body.

The sun pounds down on her head. When she reaches up to touch the sweat-stung trail on her scalp, her fingers come back flecked with gummy blood.

Earlier, she heard the stray crashing around in the sumac grove on the wrong side of the fence, had gone in after it, bending and dodging through the twisted trunks and low-hung branches until a thorn had raked across the top of her head, but this is the first attention she's paid to the feeling.

The tailgate is hot—she sits down on it anyway, takes off her boots, hangs her socks over the trailer hitch. The nails of her big toes are mashed white from being rubbed by her boots all day. She rolls up her jeans legs, studies the bruises on her shins. She knows there will be more on her thighs—dabs of dissolving pain—left by metal and wood—without registering the ache of it.

On the skyline, Old Man steps forward, bringing Davis along with him, out of the shape that melded them with Lovell and Arlee. They'll be moving now. For a moment, Ruby's head floats above the grass, then

disappears again, running low, circling and heeling, doing her part to push the bulls toward the waiting cows.

Avery waves as the men pass through the gate
and out of sight. She lies back on the hard ridges of
the pickup bed, closes her eyes. From the canyon, the
bawl of a cow—the foghorn sound of need. She thinks
of Davis's hands on her this morning and her hands on
him, the traces of whiskey still on his tongue, the light
just beginning to saturate the bedroom curtains.

Wind, creek, red-winged blackbird. Heat and hard
metal against her back. She feels the slow spin of the
earth, then the truck unmooring itself, drifting down the
hill, away from Davis and Lovell, with her in its hull, going in the direction of the sea.

piano

LOVELL'S HOUSE IS older, a different color than she remembers—wind-blasted, the color of an old chambray shirt. A line of sunflowers leans out of its shadow, burnt petals barely hanging on. Outside the shadow, the yard, gone brittle since Lennie moved to town with Wes. A locust tree, and under it, Lovell's pickup with yellow leaves scattered across its hood like coins. As Avery passes, she sees the coffee cup wedged between the windshield and dash—one of hers. She smiles.

From inside the house, the piano, a song something like a lullaby. She finds Lovell sitting on the bench, his back to her, working the pedals with his stocking feet. She stands in the doorway, recognizes the theme from *Dr. Zhivago*, pictures the album label swirling on Madeline's turntable.

Then, Lovell's hands are claws grabbing the chords to "In the Sweet Bye and Bye." She listens, pictures the upright piano in the church on Laurel Creek, the flowered kitchen curtain hung across its back to hide the workings.

Sounds like Sunday school in here, she says when he is finished.

He turns, blushes, stands.

I never heard you play before, she says. I always wanted to learn. Mom played a little, I think, but we never had a piano.

He starts to say something, pauses, then, Want some ice tea?

THREADS OF TOBACCO fall onto the kitchen table. Lovell licks the edge of the cigarette paper, rolls it between his fingers and thumbs. He pushes the cigarette between his lips, lights it with a book of matches from his pocket, inhales, pulls the cigarette away from his mouth, studies it.

Lennie tell you? he asks.

Yes, she did. Yesterday.

Bound to happen, he says. Guess I always knew she'd want to have a kid. Just surprised me, is all. He pinches a fleck of tobacco off his bottom lip, flicks it to the floor. Wes is a good guy.

The cigarette burns away into the thick haze of afternoon. Smoke mingles with dust and the burnt-egg smell in Lovell's kitchen. Outside, the shimmer of day. High summer light bounces off the chrome and glass of machinery, sticks to the bellies of locust and cottonwood leaves.

Lovell pushes the pile of tobacco around on the table with the tip of his cut finger. His wrists are thinner, translucent. Avery studies his face, realizes there is something different in the set of his eyes. They are deeper in their sockets now—not dull like Madeline's—still lit, still blue.

He jabs the cigarette butt into the bottom of an empty tuna can. You gonna be OK with this? he asks.

Yup, she says. I'm tough. You know that.

I do know that, he says. Never doubted it. He studies her. She knows he's waiting for her to say what she's come to say.

I'm going to go off for a little while, she says. Going off to Warm Springs to stay with Bernita awhile—let her teach me a little bit about catching babies.

Davis? he asks.

Avery looks at the crumb-littered linoleum, faded down to pale green, then at Lovell sitting there in his sock feet. I don't know, she says, then, Probably needs to stay here and keep you in line.

She thinks back to last night when she told Davis—his anger, her tears, the question that settled down over them like smoke, filled every corner of the house.

This makes no sense, he'd said. Why don't you just get some books, read up like you do with everything else? Maybe watch Lennie deliver a few babies. You don't have to leave to do that.

LOVELL STANDS ON the cracked sidewalk, hands in jeans pockets, watches her get into the Jeep. She smiles, says, I'll see you before I go. Then, I meant what I said about Lennie. I am happy.

Lovell nods his head, lifts one foot, then the other, steps off the cement into the cool shadow of the house, says, She's going to make a pretty good mother.

You've been a good father, Avery says.

dirt

THE BLACK ARROWHEAD shines against Avery's palm. Obsidian. She thinks to put it into her jeans pocket for Davis, pictures the marbles, shards of china and glass on the shelf above the kitchen sink, all picked out of the dirt around the place—dirt that bothers horses' eyes in summer, offers up frost-heaved stones for fence jacks, pushes up rusted hinges, nails, old wire to bother boot soles.

She thinks of a jar of arrowheads by her childhood bed, brought from the plowed fields by her father, knows they are probably still there in the pile of ashes where the house stood.

She turns it over in her palm, kneels, lays it back into the dirt.

the blue wise man

LOVELL HANDS AVERY the Wise Man, says, It's a little early, but I wanted you to have it. Finished it last night.

She turns the figure in her hands. The robe is sanded smooth, stained a pale blue. One slender hand clutches a gold box to his chest, the other, lifted in midair, as if he were about to say something. Like the others, the face is soft, almost featureless.

Thank you, she says. The first tear slips over the rim of her eye. I'm going to take him with me.

Lovell raises his eyebrows, grins.

I wanted to ask you something, she says. Madeline?

She watches his shoulders rise, hears the breath rush back out of his chest.

She wouldn't have much to do with me after Jean Ann died, he says.

How long? Avery asks.

Since before Frank . . . you . . . Jean Ann . . . Bernita. Since she came off that train with your grandma and grandpa. All those years ago.

Did Daddy know?

That, I don't know, Lovell says. I always felt kind of sorry for him. If he knew, he never said. After he left, a couple of times when she was drunk, she called me. I'd go get her . . . couple of times, then nothing ever again. I hate what's happened to her.

Why didn't you marry her before Daddy did?

I don't know, he says. Don't do no good to think about it now.

She studies Lovell's face, knows he's telling the truth—he doesn't know.

I have to go, she says.

She steps into his arms, presses the side of her face against his collarbone, the pearl snaps on his shirt, against the sweat and smoke of him, the ripe apple smell, as close as she can get to the warm, rubbed-smooth grain of him.

river

AVERY PUTS THE last bag on the back seat, closes the Jeep door. She walks to the locust tree where Davis has saddled and tied Old Man. She waits, looks around. House, barn, shed roofs gone dull in the late light.

She leans into Old Man, puts an arm around him. The smell of his neck breaks her heart.

Davis comes out of the barn—carrying nothing— walks toward them. Avery feels her body expand, contract. OK, she says to him. Time.

She watches a muscle in his jaw harden. This isn't right, he says.

I don't know what else to say, she says.

He takes a step toward her, pulls her to him. She feels the heat of his hand on the back of her head, hears him inhale once, and then again.

She makes herself stand back from him. He looks hard at her, shakes his head, looks away.

She walks to the Jeep, gets in. When she looks up, he is leading Old Man into the wheat stubble. At the fence line, he raises himself into the saddle, looks back once, waves his arm. She waves back.

The air between them shimmers, until he is a refracted thing in the distance, his shape melted into Old Man's. They are translucent and then they are gone.

By the time she pushes out of the driveway, the moon is full up—a deep water sky coming with it, and a wind that makes a sound like a river moving through the trees, a wild and invisible thing that turns them inside out.

memorial day,
warm springs reservation

THEIR HEADS NEARLY touch across the grave. Avery sits back on her heels, notices silver filaments running through Bernita's dark hair.

Cars drive up, park in the surrounding field. Reservation families walk through an opening in the wire fence, carrying rakes, garbage bags, buckets of peonies. Others, already here, kneel among the stones and wooden markers, murmuring, laughing.

Bernita looks up, smiles. She tilts her head toward the rest of the cemetery, says, Last night you watched me deliver the Alexander baby. Now you're getting the other end of things.

She drops a handful of weeds on the ground behind her, lays a hand against her mother's tombstone, says, She used to sit right here in her lawn chair—always carried a lawn chair in the trunk of her car—telling stories of the people buried here while we cleaned graves.

Bernita shifts her knees, picks at dried stems poking through the black weed barrier that covers the mound between them, says, Same stories year after year. She'd save up vases and jars—buy them at rummage sales—then go over to Madras and buy flags and plastic flowers, drag it all out here every Memorial Day. She'd sit in that chair and direct us where to put it all.

Avery shifts her tingling legs, sits back on the cold dirt, glances around. Graves piled with ceramic statues or coffee mugs or sprinkled with coins. On the way in, they'd passed a blue bicycle leaning against a hand-lettered plank, rusted, tires flat. Avery thinks about West Virginia, going to the bare family graveyard with Grandma Coleman. Vines snaking across its rocky ground. Grandma's silence, her tears.

Nearby, a grave heaped with stuffed animals. Avery shivers, pictures the Fletcher Cemetery. Months ago, the tiny mound over her baby already flattening under a blanket of fine grass. Jean Ann's grave nearby, completely level.

Bernita picks up the edge of the weed cloth, says, Lift up your side. I think we can use this again—should last another year.

As they lift the cloth, heads of tiny grass stems pop onto the black fabric. Beneath it, bugs run across the exposed dirt, trying to escape the sudden light.

They fold the barrier, lay it over the tombstone. Avery picks at the grave, pulls off more grass, flings it aside. Bernita lights a cigarette.

Avery slides her hands into the dirt, skims them just below the surface, sifts out pebbles and sticks. Cool dampness on her palms, then sharp pain across a fingertip.

Oh, she says, lifts her hand, holds up the finger. Blood rivulets down the knuckle.

Bernita picks a wedge of blue glass from the dirt, motions toward Avery's finger, says, Probably an old vase. Just let that bleed awhile. Blood will clean out the cut.

Avery holds her throbbing finger down, lets it drip, watches Bernita lay the weed barrier back over the grave then weight its edges with the rocks they'd removed earlier.

Behind Avery, a plastic pinwheel spins in a rush of wind. Bernita rummages through the cardboard box she brought, brings out a willow basket, a handful of dime store flowers.

Avery points at the basket, asks, You make that?

Make one for her every year, Bernita says, gestures toward a weed and ribbon-clotted section of fence. The one I brought last year must have blown away.

She pulls a block of green foam from the box, lays it in the basket. She pushes the metal stem of a flower into the foam, then picks through the pile of plastic blossoms, says, Mom's the one taught me. Her mother taught her how to make cornhusk bags, but Mom liked working willow better—said she liked the feel of it, the smell, so she taught me when I came back here to stay after Lovell and I split.

Oh, Avery says.

Bernita pushes another stem into the foam.

I think she thought it would help me with the pain. I missed that man so bad, and every time I looked at Lennie, I saw him—thought my heart would explode.

Avery looks down, watches a line of ants cut across the base of the tombstone, waits.

We tried to get back together once, but it didn't work. Lasted about a month. I ended up back here.

Bernita motions toward the east. Avery follows the gesture across the canyon rim, to the Plateau beyond. Home.

Avery thinks of Davis, gathering cattle today, branding tomorrow, the same as every Memorial Day since she's known him, but still he mentioned it in last week's letter, as if she would have forgotten. She wonders if he went to the cemetery early this morning before saddling up.

Bernita says, Over at Fletcher with Lovell, I was homesick. And then when I was back over here, I wanted to be over there again. It didn't make sense.

I know, Avery says. Then, Before my sister died, Mom used to talk about home, but she wasn't talking about Fletcher. She meant West Virginia.

Bernita wires the basket to a tomato stake, says, I know. I'm not sure she every really wanted to be here.

She shoves the stake into the ground near the headstone, adjusts the flowers, says, Did you know, in our language, a place can have several names, depending on where you are standing? Depends on where you look at it from.

In the car, Bernita hands Avery a paper napkin. Wrap this around your finger, she says, then she lights another cigarette, rolls down the window, says, Lennie's time is coming soon. She guesses about a week or so. You're still going over with me to help, right?

Avery feels heat rise inside her jacket. A wave of cool air enters the open window, breaks across her face. Whiff of peony and tobacco smoke.

I told Lennie I would, she says.

Bernita taps the cigarette on the doorframe. Good, she says, then, You going to stay after—help out?

Lennie asked me to, then, Where will I stay? Lennie and Wes don't have room for all of us.

Bernita scratches at a speck on the dashboard, says, Well, clinic already knows I'll be gone awhile after Lennie's baby comes. I can teach you to deliver babies over there same as here. Where you stay is up to you.

lennie

ENNIE INHALES, LIFTS her head off Wes's chest, drops her chin. She grunts, digs her fingers into the backs of her thighs. The baby's head moves further out, then recedes, a drifting boat pulled back to the shore.

Almost there, Bernita says. She turns to look at Avery, moves aside, says to her, Come help me. We'll do this together.

In the doorway, Lovell's voice, then Davis's. Low, serious. Avery meets Davis's eyes. Smiles at him, feels her stomach unanchor.

Lennie lifts her head again, squeezes her eyes closed, pushes, looks at her mother. Avery leans further into the tub. With stuttering fingers, she traces a whorl of dark hair on the baby's crown before it disappears again.

Avery feels Lennie's thighs stiffen, tremble.

This time, Lennie says. She closes her eyes, grimaces, grunts. Avery opens her hands, feels the baby's head drop into her palms—a mossy stone. Breathe, Lennie, she says, then, One more time.

The baby slides out into the water, a luminescent fish. Avery feels the weight of him rising off her hands, grips him tighter, lifts. He breaks the plane of the water, opens his eyes, breathes.